The Watercress Farm

Kay Seeley

Published by Enterprise Books

Copyright © 2023 Kay Seeley

ISBN 978914592-13-3

All author and publisher proceeds from the sale of this book will be donated to the reSEND CIC Pay it Forward Fund to support parents and carers of children with Special Educational Needs.

reSEND CIC is a Non-profit Independent SEN Advisory Service.

Chapter One

Jessie sat at the solid oak kitchen table, the morning post spread before her. She recognised the envelopes. They were all bills. She took a sip of her extra strong espresso and braced herself for what the letter in her hand might contain. The logo of her bank was displayed on the envelope. Her jaw tightened. She put her coffee cup down and slit the envelope open, carefully withdrawing its contents.

She flicked the letter open and scanned the page. Hot blood flushed her cheeks. She knew things had been difficult for a while, but had only recently learned the full extent of her father's financial problems. She'd had a lot of extra expenses too, what with the funeral and everything. She was trying to struggle on for his sake, but she wasn't sure how long she could put off the reckoning that had to come. It seemed as though the bank felt the same.

Something nudged her leg. She glanced down and saw Lady, her father's Labrador staring back at her, her chocolate brown eyes pleading. She smiled and rubbed Lady's head, the way she knew Lady liked. "Want to go out? Come on then." She shoved the letter in her pocket, but couldn't stop tears welling up in her eyes as she rose and opened the farmhouse door to let Lady out.

Outside the morning sun dappled the grass and shimmered on the silvery strips of water where the emerald green watercress grew. Her heart crunched as she glanced around at the watercress beds that had provided a living for her family for generations. They meant more to her than a way of making a living. This was her home. All her childhood memories were tied up in this place. This is where she'd grown up, where she'd taken her first toddler steps, had her first pony and learned to ride. This is where her love of life and horses had begun. Was this to be the end of the line?

Her first pony was called Barney, and she'd loved him with a passion. Every morning she'd be at the stable grooming him and it was the first place she'd run to after school. Long summer holidays were spent riding Barney in the paddock and over the jumps.

Of course, it wasn't all fun. She'd had to work as well. She'd worked in the watercress beds, learning the secrets of growing the best cress, retaining the seed for next year's sowing. Cutting it and keeping it fresh until it went to market.

She'd loved working with her father listening to his tales of when he was growing up around the same watercress beds. She loved hearing how his father had told him about growing cress during the war when it provided vital vitamins and minerals while food was on ration. "It weren't a proper tea without cress sandwiches on the table," her grandfather used to say. He told her how the Generals in Roman times used to feed cress to their soldiers as it was rumoured to 'give them vigour'. They both chuckled at that. They were happy days of sunshine and laughter. A shiver of memory ran though her. It was no use reliving the past. It was the future she needed to worry about now. The letter from the bank burned in her pocket.

Lady did her usual round, sniffing at the tufts of grass that grew around the bare mud of the driveway. Then Jessie saw Ned, the farmhand who'd been with her father for as long as she could remember. He'd come to cut the cress ready to take to the market. She watched him crossing the yard, his back slightly bent, his gait slower than she remembered. She waved and he smiled and waved back. His hair may be grey, but his smile was just as cheery. She grimaced. What would happen to Ned if she lost the farm?

Lady came bouncing up to her again. She fussed the dog. "Come on in then, let's get you sorted."

Inside she filled Lady's bowls with food and fresh water, tidied the pile of bills away and swigged back the last of her coffee. She rinsed the cup under the tap and put them to drain on the board next to the sink. Glancing in the mirror she pulled her thick chestnut hair back swinging it expertly into a ponytail. She bit her lip, made a face at herself and laughed. Who was she trying to impress? She was only going to the market.

Once Lady had finished her meal Jessie moved her water bowl outside. "You'll have to stay out until I get back," she said, ushering Lady out of the door. She ruffled her ears and sighed. "It's all right for you old girl, at least you get to lie in the sun. I'll be on my feet all day."

Inside she picked up her bag and coat, pulled on her wellington boots, went out and closed the door. Ned had finished loading the crates of watercress into the back of the pick-up truck ready for her to take to her neighbours, Tom and Mary. He opened the gate as Jessie drove out.

Mary greeted her at the door as she drove up. "You're early," she said. "Tom's just gone to fetch the cheeses. Have you got time for a cuppa?"

Jessie sank into a chair at the well-worn kitchen table. Copper pans hanging over the iron range reflected the early morning sunlight. The bright, cosiness of the kitchen cheered her. Here she would find only friendship and support. Mary poured her tea from the huge brown teapot. Jessie took the letter out of her pocket and passed it to Mary. "It's from the bank," she said. "They want me to make an appointment with their Small Business Adviser. You don't need to be a genius to know what that's all about."

Mary sat and read the letter. "Oh dear," she said. "Tom deals with all that sort of thing." She handed the letter back to Jessie. "He did say there'd been a lot of changes at the bank recently. New broom and all that. The new chap wanting to make his mark I expect."

"Probably a black mark as far as I'm concerned," Jessie said with a grimace. "Things have been piling up recently, I need to make some changes myself if I'm to survive."

"Well, perhaps that's all the bank need to know. What plans you have for the future."

Jessie shrugged. "I wish I knew."

"If there's anything we can do..."

"No, it's all right you've done enough. Letting me sell my cress alongside your cheeses helps. That and always being here."

Mary poured herself another cup of tea. "It must have been hard, coming home to find how bad things were with your dad being so ill."

Jessie sighed. The memory of her father's illness brought a stab of pain. She missed him every day. It was his illness brought her home from Andalucía. An illness she'd have known nothing about if it hadn't been for Mary keeping in touch. A chatty e-mail arrived every couple of weeks and Jessie and Mary had even chatted over the internet, exchanging news, exchanges Jessie valued as they brought home closer. It was Mary who'd told her about her dad's illness. Stubborn as the mule that pulled the pony cart, her dad hadn't wanted to bother her. He obviously hadn't wanted to bother her with details of his dire financial position either.

Her jaw clenched at the memory. Still, she was glad she'd come home. It was the right time, for more reasons than one. She couldn't regret it, but things hadn't worked out the way she'd hoped. It was three months since the funeral and the ache was still raw.

"He was a good man, your dad. One of the best," Mary said.

"I know."

"Still, you gave him a good send off. Must have cost you a packet. Is that why you're in trouble now?"

"It's what he deserved," Jessie said, unexpected tears welling up in her eyes. "He deserved the best."

"I know love, but still…" Mary paused before she spoke again. "You could always sell up, you know. Take the money and run. No one would blame you."

"No, I'd never do that."

"It's something to think about though, isn't it? If push comes to shove and you can't manage. Developers have bought the old Cosby place. Paid a good price too so I heard. And they're looking to buy more land."

"Developers? What sort of development could they put up there? It's a bit off the beaten track."

Mary shrugged. "I don't know. Just developers. Tom reckons it's a wind farm. Not much use putting anything else up there."

Tom arrived just in time to hear the end of the conversation. "Wouldn't mind one of them wind turbines myself," he said. "Save the cost of our electricity."

"We don't get enough wind down here," Mary said. "Have to go up the hill for that."

"Aye. They get the view and the wind, we get the water. Isn't that right, Jessie?" Tom said.

Jessie laughed. Tom was right about the water. It was the spring water that flowed through her property that had let her four times great grandfather plant the watercress beds that gave the farm its name and had kept them fed for over a hundred years.

"Get away with you, Tom," Mary said. "Still, it's a thought. The developers will pay a good price, far more than the current value as it stands. It's all business with them. Memories and tradition don't pay the bills."

"Not something I'm prepared to think about right now," Jessie said putting her cup back on the saucer and standing up ready to leave.

"All loaded ready for market," Tom said, realising Jessie had heard enough about the subject. "Are you sure you can manage on your own? I could come if you like."

"No, I'll be fine. Taking my turn running the stall is the least I can do when you're paying for it." To Jessie selling her cress alongside their speciality cheeses was a lifesaver. The bulk of the crop went to the processing plant the other side of town, to be put in bags with other salad leaves, but the income from the market was the jam that went on the bread, or always had been. Now, with receipts dwindling, the future looked bleak.

As she drove to the market Jessie couldn't help thinking about what Mary had said. So, Holly Berry Farm, old Mr Cosby's place, had been sold at last. It had been on the market for a while. Still, it'd be interesting to see what the developers paid for it. Not that she was thinking of selling up. She'd promised her dad.

She fingered the gold pendant around her neck, a horseshoe entwined with a sprig of watercress. Her father had had it made for her when she left to take up the job she'd been offered in Spain. "So, you don't forget where you come from," he'd said. As if she could.

He'd been so proud of her. "Your mum would have been proud too," he said with tears in his eyes. Although his wife had died when Jessie was in her teens, he'd always spoken about her as if she was still there – telling Jessie what she would have thought and would have said. It was his way of keeping her memory alive.

Jessie smiled at the sliver of memory. Those last few months looking after her dad had been traumatic. Watching him fade away was almost more than she could bear. Sitting with him night after night they'd talked more in those few months than Jessie could ever recall.

She'd tell him about the people at the market and how well the cress was selling. He'd talk about the old days, when he was a boy. Then sadness would fill his eyes.

"I should have done more," he'd say. "I've let things go. I wasn't practical like your mum. She was the one with all the ideas, the one who got things done. I was too much of a dreamer. Thought I could do it all on my own." He'd lapse into silence and Jessie would take his hand.

"Don't worry," she'd say. "I'll sort something out. I won't sell the farm."

"Don't think you have to keep it on my account. You have to chase your own dreams, not mine and your mum's. Don't be shackled to the past like I've been. Go out and live your own life, your own way. Your mum would say that too. She'd want you to be happy."

The last thing Jessie remembered him saying before he passed away was, "Follow your heart, Jessie. It won't lead you astray."

But where was her heart? She'd lost it in Spain and had it broken. A vision of Carlos Rodriguez's face ran through her mind, clear as if he's been sitting next to her. She could almost smell the warm spicy smell of him on the breeze that came in through the open window. She shook her head to dispel the memory.

She'd come home for good. There was no going back. She wanted to make a new beginning, but how could she let the farm that had been her family's home and living for generations go? She couldn't.

Luke Chambers picked up his black leather over-night bag and stepped down from the train. He glanced around. The platform was empty, the station appeared deserted. Frowning he made his way out onto the dusty forecourt.

He'd taken the slow train north as the fast didn't stop at Netherdean. Looking around he could see why. "Just get the feel of the place," his father said when he sent him. Well, so far, his first impression was of shabby, faded gentility. The style of the station told him it was late Victorian and had once been an icon of nineteenth-century splendour. Outside, faded pink and cream paint flaked and peeled on the ornate mouldings. A trough of pink and mauve flowers stood either side of the oak door. So someone had made an effort to brighten the place up, he thought.

He sniffed the air; sweeter and fresher than the grimy, smoke-filled London air. He smelled – what was it? Lavender? Roses? Whatever it was it reminded him of freshly washed sheets and pillows, sunlight streaming through nursery windows and Nanny, buxom, white aproned Nanny, who had looked after him in his early years, before he was sent away to school.

He smiled and shook the memories away. He'd been here less than five minutes and already his mind was wandering, but that's what this place felt like – like stepping back into a fondly remembered past.

A shiny black limousine swept into the forecourt and came to a stop in front of him. The car, like the station, was vintage and had seen better days. A man wearing a grey suit jumped out, tipped his peaked cap and said, "Mr Chambers?"

Luke must have nodded, he wasn't sure, but the man hurried round, took his bag and carried it to the waiting car. Within seconds they were on their way, driving through narrow streets lined with a hotch-potch of odd shaped buildings spanning centuries of style. Some were half-timbered Tudor, others Georgian or Medieval Roman inspired. All appeared rickety and crowded like a row of mismatched dining chairs. Quaint was the word that sprung to mind, but he felt sure that quaintness hadn't featured in his father's proposed development.

His father had bought the land at auction, sight unseen. "A good acreage. Enough for at least fifty houses," he'd said. "Possibly more if we go for multi-occupancy dwellings. Get our money back in no time." Looking around now Luke wasn't so sure.

When they arrived at the hotel it looked comfortable enough. Thick carpets covered the floor and a plaque on the wall announced that the building dated from the sixteenth century. Luke didn't doubt that. He didn't intend to stay for more than one night. It was miles from anywhere and it wouldn't take him long to sus out the viability of his father's plans. He still couldn't understand what possessed his usually cautious father to buy a piece of land so far out of town. It had taken him three hours on the slow train. Too far out to commute and it didn't look as though there was much in the way of industry here either. His father had said it was once a bustling market town. Well, he couldn't see any evidence of that now. Perhaps there were hidden possibilities he'd missed, but he doubted it.

He registered and when the elderly porter arrived to carry his bag, he recognised him as the driver of the car that had collected him from the station. He led Luke up the narrow stairway and along a creaky corridor. The room he showed him into was small, but the bed was large and looked inviting after his journey.

He sighed, tipped the porter and went to check out the facilities.

A freshly painted blue and white bathroom had been made out of an adjoining room. Luke was pleased to see the modern, obviously new shower unit, but a smile crossed his face at the other fittings. He couldn't remember when he'd last seen crosshead taps that you actually had to turn on and a toilet with a chain to pull to flush. Again, the feeling of having stepped back in time washed over him.

He started to unpack his things. He laid his laptop on the dressing table, opened it and searched for a socket to plug it in. A vision of the rows of plugs with instant Wi-Fi access in the modern hotels he usually stayed in ran through his mind. They were geared to meet the needs of businessmen on the move with fast, efficient service their watchword. This place was certainly different. He had to unplug the table lamp before he could plug in his laptop. Then he saw the notice declaring that *'Wi-Fi is available'* and instructing him to *'Enquire at Reception'.* Shaking his head he closed his laptop and took out his phone to text his father that he had arrived.

May sunshine shone in through net curtained windows. He had a meeting with the estate agent tomorrow, until then he might as well try to make the most of his time to find out more about the town and the farmland his father planned to develop. He was here to do a job and do it he would. Then he could go safely back to London and get on with his life.

He changed out of his business suit and pulled on a pair of jeans and a rugby shirt. He hung his suit in the wardrobe. Then he wandered downstairs and out into the sunshine.

Chapter Two

Bright sunlight lit up the summer blue sky as Jessie arrived at the market. A light breeze fluttered the colourful striped canvases stretched over the stalls. The hum of the burger vans setting up, their motors running, added to the general noise and bustle of the market. The smell of bacon and burgers hung in the air. Several of the traders were already at their stalls and Jessie exchanged a cheery 'good morning' as she unloaded the crates of cress.

She unpacked Tom and Mary's cold shelf and set out the cheeses and bunches of watercress. It was how her father and grandfather used to sell it. Not in plastic bags mixed with other leaves like the supermarket. Her grandfather would be spinning in his grave. She smiled at the memory of those childhood days when she'd toddle alongside him, nibbling at the cress as they walked around the farm. "Best food in the world," he'd say. Happy days, she thought, which brought her again to recall the letter in her pocket. It was no use putting it off. As Mary had said earlier, "It's not like flu, love. It won't go away if you ignore it."

She took out her phone and rang the bank to make an appointment for the following day.

The market was busy, and Jessie enjoyed talking to the people who stopped by the stall. She'd explain to them about the different cheeses Mary had on offer and say how well they'd go with the cress. She knew most of the locals who stopped and bought their cress and cheese from the stall.

Mrs Bagley, the cook at the hotel, stopped by. "We've a chap coming in from London," she said. "Only staying the one night, but I want to cook something special. Don't want 'im thinking we don't know how to cater for sophisticated tastes."

Jessie smiled. "You could try Mum's watercress soup," she said. She'd printed out a number of her mother's recipes and was generous in handing them out to customers who bought cress. She handed one to Mrs Bagley. "Served cold it's a lovely summer soup. You can't go wrong with that as a starter."

"Great," Mrs Bagley said taking up several bunches. "I knew I could rely on you." She walked away with a beaming smile on her face.

The morning went quickly as Jessie found she was kept busy explaining the different cheeses and what people could do with the cress. It was almost time for lunch when she saw Billy Marks standing next to the stall, watching her. She remembered Billy from school. He was a bit of a daredevil, always in trouble and his mum and dad were often up the school sorting him out.

After leaving school he'd done various jobs, none of which ever lasted very long, before settling down, getting married and taking over his father's estate agency in the village. Word was he'd had a bit of a chequered past, but Jessie wasn't one to rely too much on gossip. She knew well enough how that could get out of hand. She hadn't seen him since she left Netherdean five years ago, yet, here he was, large as life staring at her.

"Hello Billy," she said. "I haven't seen you in the market before. What brings you to our neck of the woods?"

"Not really my scene," he said, "but I wanted to check a few things out."

"Oh, I see. And my watercress was one of those things?"

"Not exactly." He smiled and Jessie remembered how mischievous he was, and how that magical smile hid a multitude of sins. "I heard you'd come home when your dad was ill. I wanted to say how sorry I was to hear of his passing."

A shiver of memory ran down Jessie's spine. "That's kind of you," she said.

"I was sorry to have missed the funeral. Quite an event from what I hear, with the whole village turning out."

"Yes, people were very kind."

"He was well liked and one of the good guys," Billy said.

Jessie nodded. Their conversation was interrupted by a customer looking for a seriously strong cheese. Jessie was quickly able to point her in the right direction.

"So, you're on your own now?" Billy asked, eyebrows raised.

"It would seem so." Jessie began to wonder what he was getting at. Mary had kept her up to date with all the comings and goings in the village while she was working in Andalucía. She'd heard about Billy's marriage troubles and eventual divorce. It seemed that he was on his own too.

An elderly lady with a brown and white terrier on a lead stopped at the stall. She couldn't make up her mind which cheese she wanted. "My sister's coming to tea and I did so want to cook her something special," she said. "She did a Cordon Bleu course and thinks she's a better cook than me."

Jessie showed her some of her mother's recipes. "What about a double-baked two cheese soufflé served with a watercress salad?" Jessie said. "The peppery freshness of the watercress balances the strong taste of the cheese."

"How lovely," the old lady said. "This'll impress her. Just the ticket."

Jessie smiled as another happy customer walked away.

Billy was still standing next to the stall, watching the transaction, shuffling from one foot to the other.

"Was it watercress or cheese you were after?" Jessie asked. "Or both?" Her emerald green eyes widened.

"Er – no – well, okay. I'll take some of each, but I was wondering if you'd like to come out for a drink."

Jessie's stomach crunched. That was the last thing she'd expected. Billy was all right, he was an old friend, but she couldn't imagine him ever being more than that.

"I don't know," she said. "I have to get these cheeses back and sort out the stall."

Billy looked put out. "It's up to you," he said. "No pressure. Just a quick drink to talk over old times. I don't expect you get out much, what with the farm to run and everything."

That was true enough.

"I'll think about it," she said, trying to make it sound as non-committal as possible.

He shrugged. "I'll be in The Feathers from six o'clock if you decide to join me."

She nodded. "Fine."

Still, he was right. The months looking after her father had brought them closer, but now he was gone there was a huge void in her life. Perhaps going out for a drink with Billy would go a little way to filling it. She could catch up with the rest of the world and get back into the swing of things. Perhaps it was time.

Once Luke stepped out into the sunshine his mood lifted. The walk to the High Street was pleasant and a good variety of shops piqued his interest. There was a library and a substantial looking Town Hall. He passed a horse trough, a post office and a war memorial, everything you'd expect to see in a thriving market town

Walking around Luke tried to imagine the sort of development his father planned and how it would impact on this curiously appealing town. The first thing he noticed was how people stopped in the street to chat. Everyone appeared to know everyone else and they never passed without a smile and a cheery greeting. An image of Oxford Street in rush-hour, shoppers battling, heads down, along crowded pavements, filled his mind, so different from these people sauntering along as though they had all the time in the world.

His first port-of-call was the local pub where he thought he might try their 'Special Lunch Deal' advertised on a sandwich-board propped up on the pavement.

Stepping inside it took a while for his eyes to become accustomed to the sudden darkness. He'd had to duck to avoid hitting his head on one of the solid oak beams that stretched across the low ceiling. Dim light came in through tiny, curtained windows while lamps around the walls gave off dull amber glows, despite it being the middle of the day. The musty smell of beer and sweat filled the air. Tables and chairs were grouped around plush, red-upholstered benches in alcoves around the room. The only occupants were two elderly men sat in a corner playing cribbage.

"Morning sir," a florid faced, sturdy barman greeted him. "What's your pleasure today?"

He ordered a pint and a ploughman's lunch, paid and sat at one of the tables, feeling as out of place as a fish in a flowerpot. At home he'd have had his lunch in a light, airy wine bar, all chrome and glass, buzzing with people and conversation. Once again, he wondered at his father's decision to buy land in this remote, rural area. What on earth was he thinking?

He shook his head. As he ate his lunch he thought about his father. He recalled his strong decisive nature and how everything he touched turned into what he called 'brass'. It was his father's business acumen, and his property development company, Stone's Homes, that had allowed Luke to go to a good school, follow his passion and study Architecture all over the world. Had he lost his touch?

After lunch Luke noticed people going to and from the nearby market. The smell of burgers and onions from a van parked at the entrance hung in the air. The afternoon sun sparkled on the colourful striped canvasses flapping in the light breeze.

He wondered if it'd be any different from the London markets, famous for the huge variety of wares and the outgoing personalities of the stallholders.

Walking around he noticed the freshness of the produce, everything from potatoes to salad leaves just that morning picked or dug up from the soil that still clung to them. He thought of his friend Henri, the chef at his club. How he'd love the chance to buy such fresh from the ground food. He meandered through the stalls, stopping to gaze at what was on offer. There seemed to be plenty of people around too.

He was just thinking of making his way back to the hotel when he saw the cheese stall, or rather the girl behind the stall. She was chatting to an elderly lady and laughing. Strands of deep chestnut hair had escaped from her ponytail to frame her delicate features. Her eyes sparkled when she laughed, and her smile lit up her face like a shaft of sunshine. Most girls of his acquaintance wouldn't be seen dead without being immaculately made up and wearing the latest designer outfit. This girl had not a scrap of make up on and wore a blue check blouse tucked into faded jeans. She still took his breath away. She was the loveliest girl he'd ever seen.

His heart beat a little faster. Perhaps there was more to this place than he had previously supposed.

That afternoon, at about four o'clock Jessie packed up the stall and drove back to Mary's to drop off the unsold cheeses.

"Can you or Tom man the stall tomorrow," she asked. "I have an appointment at the bank."

"I'll do it," Mary said. "Fingers crossed it goes it goes all right for you. Best to get it sorted anyway."

Jessie nodded.

Back at home she put the few bunches of left-over cress with the cress to go to the processing plant in the morning. Then she changed into a fresh blouse and clean jeans. She brushed her chestnut hair loose and put on a dash of lipstick. She finished with a spritz of the perfume she'd bought at the duty free on the way home from Spain. The spicy fragrance brought a maelstrom of memories which she quickly brushed away. Tears blurred her vision as she drove out to go to the pub to meet Billy.

By six o'clock The Feathers was busy and crowded with customers. Billy steered her to a table under the window and bought her a glass of wine.

"How are you getting on?" he asked. "It can't be easy being on your own."

"It's not," she said. "But I manage. Ned's a great help. He practically runs the place."

"Ah, yes, Ned. Still, he must be getting on. How much longer do you think he'll be around to help out?"

Jessie's brow creased into a frown. "What do you mean? That's not very nice. Ned's fine. He's fit as a fiddle."

Billy blushed. "Sorry, I only meant he must be past sixty by now. Maybe he'd like a chance to retire and sit back."

Jessie's heart stuttered. Billy was right. Ned was getting on. Was she being unfair, expecting him to carry on doing the work he'd always done?

"Well, he hasn't said anything," she managed.

"No, but think about it, Jessie. If you were to sell the farm you could go back to your life in Spain and he could spend his final years pottering around in his garden. It'd suit you both."

A volcano of anger exploded inside Jessie. "Sell the farm? Is that why you asked me out for a drink? So you could pressure me into selling the farm and making you a nice commission?" Hot blood flushed her face.

"No, not the only reason, but you know there are property developers…"

He didn't get any further. Jessie stood and glared at him. "You know what you can do with your drink and any ideas you may have about me selling up." She picked up her wine, threw it in his face and slammed the glass down on the table before storming out.

Outside she shook with rage. How stupid she'd been to think that Billy might be interested in her, not the farm. A wave of ferocious fury washed over her. What did she expect? He was like all the men she knew, only after what he could get out of her. She clenched her jaw. Why had she been so gullible? She blinked away the tears that threatened to fall. She'd take more care where she placed her hopes and dreams in the future. Then she remembered the letter from the bank and her heart sank to her boots. Had she done the right thing telling Billy she wasn't interested in selling up? Would the bank force her to?

Chapter Three

When she got home from the disastrous 'date' with Billy, Jessie went into her father's study. She'd avoided going in there since he'd died, preferring to do her bookwork on the kitchen table, but now she wanted to go through his papers. She glanced around the room. Memories flooded her brain. This had always been such a happy place. Her dad had sat behind that desk, puffing away at his pipe, just as his father and grandfather had before him.

The photos lined up along the wall of her mum and dad, grandfather and great grandfather brought a smile to her face and a curious feeling of wellbeing. Seeing them, all there together, looking so proud, she felt a great sense of continuity. She was sure they'd encountered many difficulties in their lives too, but with courage and determination they'd overcome them. Now it was her turn to do the same.

It took her over an hour to go through the papers. She found plans her parents had drawn up many years ago to turn the farmhouse into a B & B and the barn into a petting farm. Pony or tractor rides would be an added attraction. She recalled her mother talking with great enthusiasm about it, before she succumbed to the illness that finally took her. Jessie was about fifteen then. After that, her dad lost heart and nothing ever became of it. It was as he'd said, her mum was the one with the ideas and the enthusiasm to carry them through. After she died he lost interest and seemed to drift like a ship without anchor. It was as though he'd given up, but then carried on for Jessie's sake and the debt owed to his forefathers. That was when their sheep and cows had gone and the fields had been rented out. He was right when he said he'd been shackled by the past. Jessie realised that now.

Eventually she found her father's financial papers. Her legs turned to jelly and she sank into the chair when she saw the extent of the debts owed to the bank. As well as the huge overdraft there was evidence of a loan taken out over a year ago. She wondered how that had been repaid, or, if indeed it had been.

As she went through the papers, she became more and more exasperated. How had her father allowed things to get into such a state? It was obvious her mum was the practical one. He'd just bumbled along hoping for the best and ignoring the worse. The accounts were well out of date with no entries since she came home from Spain, almost as though he couldn't face what he would find by keeping the books. Oh Dad, she thought more than once, how could you? Then she reminded herself how ill he'd been and her anger faded into helplessness. If only she'd known, she could have helped.

It became clear that keeping the farm running without making some drastic changes was no longer an option. She'd have to think of something else. She'd have to find another way of supporting herself and Ned. The money from the cress and the income from two fields rented out to a neighbour for grazing his sheep, wouldn't go anywhere near the amount needed to satisfy the bank.

She'd given up a promising career at a stud farm in Andalucía to come home to nurse her father. She'd learned a lot about business in the five years she was there. Now she intended to put her experience to good use. Mary and Billy had both mentioned developers building on Holly Berry Farm, the old Cosby place. Developers meant houses, houses meant people, people meant customers and the possibility of expanding her business to offer more than watercress. She had the barns, byres and outbuildings, long standing empty and unused. Well perhaps now it was time to start over and make use of her assets.

Vincent Sowerbridge, the newest member of staff at Netherdean branch of the bank, checked his morning appointment. He noticed an entry for Jessie Tyler at eleven. His lips spread into a smile. Everyone at the bank had heard about the sale of Holly Berry Farm to London based property developers, Stone's Homes. He, himself, had heard Billy Marks, the local estate agent, bragging about it in the pub. Out of interest he'd checked the map and seen that Watercress Farm lay directly between Holly Berry Farm and the main road. It didn't take a genius to work out that the extra acreage and road access would make Watercress Farm a prime target for the developers.

He'd cursed his luck when he'd been posted to Netherdean, a small rural branch in the middle of nowhere where everyone knew everyone else's business and felt entitled to tittle-tattle it around the town. If you had an egg for breakfast when you got to work everyone would ask if you enjoyed it. It was a hotbed of rumour and gossip which he could now use to his advantage.

He found out everything he could about Jessie Tyler. He spent long lunch hours in the pub, eves-dropping on other people's conversations. He learned that Jessie had given up a good job with a promising career at a stud farm in Andalucía to come home and look after her ailing father. Now he was gone she'd inherited the farm. The impression was that, with farming being so hard with little reward, her best bet would be to give it all up and go back to Spain. At least he hoped that was true.

He checked the Watercress Farm account at the bank and was delighted to see such a high deficit. That should make his job easier. He'd left his last place under a cloud. Complaints had been made about his methods. In order to increase his commission he'd agreed loans to people who were clearly unable to replay them, resulting in default, repossession and recovery of the debt through administration and bankruptcy: an expensive process which didn't always result in full recovery, and which gave the bank a bad name. He was accused of being irresponsible. True he'd been careless, slapdash even, this time it would be different. If he could land Stone's Homes' account for the bank it would be bonuses all round and possibly promotion. Watercress Farm could be his means to that end. If he could secure the property for Stone's Homes, who knew where he may end up? A post in London perhaps? It would be a dream come true.

The next morning, after a full English breakfast, Luke picked up his briefcase and camera and headed out to where Billy Marks was waiting to take him to the farmland his father had bought, sight unseen. He wasn't sure what he expected to see. The picture and description on the internet, advertising the land for sale, stuck in his mind, but he'd been to enough sites to know the pictures painted didn't always match the reality.

Driving out of town the road became less congested. Cars and lorries gave way to farm vehicles and trucks. Trees lined the route, flashes of sunlight reaching through their branches. Everywhere appeared green in the morning sunshine. They drove between high hedges and trees that had stood for a hundred years. The countryside had an ageless permanence about it, as though their journey through it would leave no impression, like the train that sped through green hills on the way there, underlining man's insignificance.

The tranquillity of the countryside had an unexpected effect on Luke. As they drove through a tunnel of shade formed by the trees aching overhead, he felt himself shrouded in an eerie silence. His shoulders dropped of their own accord as the tension of the morning left them. Calm fell over him. His breathing deepened and his heart slowed.

Eventually they turned off the road along a dirt track. When they reached the farm Billy stopped the car and got out to open the gate. Luke smiled, he needn't have bothered. The gate fell off its hinges as he tried to push it open. Scowling Billy picked up the pieces of worn, weathered wood, and threw them aside. Then he drove Luke up to the farmhouse.

Luke got out of the car and stood and stared. The picture on the advert must have been taken decades before. The building in front of him bore little resemblance to the photo.

He leaned into the car to retrieve his camera and briefcase. Lifting the camera, he took a picture of the building. The front door and windows were dusty with cobwebs. Then he turned to survey the view from the house which stretched right across the valley. It was stunning. It appeared as though a patchwork quilt had been laid over the landscape. Green, sheep-spotted fields sat alongside squares in varying shades of brown and yellow. Watching white winged birds follow a tractor in the distance he was filled with a sense of timeless continuity where the landscape endlessly changed with the seasons, yet remained the same. The only thing changing was his own perception.

"If you want to go in, I've got the keys," Billy said, shaking Luke out of his reverie.

Luke smiled. "Yes please."

Billy fumbled with the keys until he found the right one, then pushed the door open. The smell of must and dust filled Luke's nostrils. It was obviously a long time since anyone had visited the house.

Inside Billy led him to the kitchen. A large wooden butcher's table stood in the centre of the room. Along one wall a dilapidated range stood alongside an abandoned dresser. The walls were stained with a lifetime's accumulation of grease and dirt.

Luke's camera clicked.

"We never said it was immaculate," Billy said, looking uncomfortable and shuffling his feet. "Has prospects we said. Never made any promises."

Luke took a breath. He took an Ordinance Survey map out of his briefcase and spread it out on the table. "Show me where the boundaries are," he said and handed Billy a blue marker.

Billy leaned over the map and outlined an area containing fields and a good sized area of forest. Luke bridled. That would be a problem. You couldn't just go cutting down ancient woodlands, he knew that.

Gazing at the map he noticed the surrounding areas were all farms. The dirt track they'd come along was the only exit to the main road. Below Holly Berry Farm another farm lay between it and the road.

"What's that?" Luke asked.

"Ah," Billy said. "Good spot. That's Watercress Farm. The old man who ran it died recently. We may be able to get the extra land for you, at a price."

Luke's lips thinned as he pressed them together. It was true the extra land would be a useful addition to the plot, but he wasn't going to pay through the nose for it. He'd met a lot of sharks and wheeler dealers in his time. People trying to hold you over a barrel for inflated prices. It was a road he had no intention of going down.

Luke took photos of the other downstairs rooms, the hall and stairs and the three large bedrooms, with a disgruntled Billy following on his heels. All looked dusty and forsaken. He glanced out of an upstairs window. The view took his breath away. If I lived here I'd never want to leave, he thought.

"Who lived here before?" he asked.

"Old Mr Cosby," Billy said. "He farmed dairy and crops. His sons fell out over the farm, that's why it was left empty for so long. Now one's in Australia and the other in America. They wanted it sold as quickly as possible, which is why we put it up for auction and you got it at a rock bottom price."

Luke nodded. It was just as his father had told him.

Outside he took photos of the meadow, now ablaze with wildflowers and wandered down to the woods where a carpet of bluebells scented the air. Again, he had a feeling of wellbeing, of the timeless continuity of it and of not wanting to disturb or change anything.

He tried to imagine the sort of development his father planned here, in this beautiful, peaceful place, but he couldn't. The vision just wouldn't come.

"And you said there was planning permission?" he asked Billy who was following him around like a besotted puppy.

"Well, no. We never said that." Billy said. "What we said was it may be possible."

"Possible? So, what does that mean?"

"It means that a well-known developer like Stone's Homes, with contacts and resources, would, in all probability, be able to arrange it."

Luke's jaw tightened. "Contacts and resources? What exactly do you mean by that?"

Billy grinned and his face twisted into what wasn't exactly a nod and a wink, but, in Luke's view was more than half-way there. "You know. Money talks and all that."

"I hope you're not suggesting what I think you're suggesting," Luke said.

Billy's eyes widened and he shrugged. Luke's heart hardened. From where he was standing it looked as though his father had been sold the land under false pretences. There was no way they could develop the land, nor, now he'd seen it, would Luke want to. The best thing they could do would be to cut their losses and put it back on the market -- unless...

The idea came to him so suddenly he almost dismissed it, but it wouldn't budge. Looking around he could see it. It was a great idea, and it would solve all their problems, but could he get this father to agree?

Chapter Four

The next morning Jessie dropped the crates of watercress off at the market with Mary and went into town. She'd sat up all night trying to work out a way to save the farm. She'd had a few ideas and jotted them down. Perhaps the business adviser could help flesh out the possibilities. It was the only way she could see to save the farm.

Walking into the bank sent a shiver down her spine. Behind the counter the cashiers sat nonchalantly dealing with customers. There was a short queue, mostly farmers come in on their weekly visit to bank their takings or draw out cash for wages. Jessie went up to the desk marked 'Information'.

"I'd like to see," she checked the name on the letter, "Mr Vincent Sowerbridge, the Small Business Adviser."

The girl on the desk smiled. "Please take a seat."

Jessie sat. It felt like hours, but was probably not more than ten minutes. Some special kind of torture that bank staff invent to put you on edge, she thought, remembering what her dad said he'd felt whenever he came to the bank. She sat twiddling her thumbs, gazing around with the speech she planned to make, and the proposition she'd come up with during the long night, running through her head. This was the last chance saloon. She knew that. A stone of anxiety lodged in her stomach. She took a breath.

The phone on the desk rang. The girl answered it. "Mr Sowerbridge will see you now," she said.

Jessie rose to be greeted by a man in a pin-striped suit. His fair hair was slicked back, beady eyes stared at her from his narrow, pinched face. He stretched out his hand. "Good morning," he said. "I'm Vincent Sowerbridge, Small Business Adviser."

Jessie's heart sank to her boots. Mr Sowerbridge didn't look the sort of man who'd have any sympathy with a woman struggling to retain her heritage. She followed him into the office, trying to remain optimistic. She needed to get him on her side to get the funding for the expansion of the farm that she planned.

The office was cold and efficient. Venetian blinds sent slats of light onto a grey metal desk. Vincent Sowerbridge gave an unconvincing smile as he seated himself behind it. Mary's words about a new chap wanting to make his mark echoed in Jessie's head, and the carefully rehearsed words of her prepared speech flew from her mind like migrating birds.

"Now, what can we do for you today?" Vincent asked.

"I've had this letter," Jessie said, taking it out of her bag and thrusting it in front of him.

"Hmm, I see." He tapped the keyboard in front of him to bring Jessie's account up on his computer. His eyebrows shot up to his hairline and Jessie was sure she saw a flicker of glee shine briefly in his eyes before his face assembled itself into a serious expression.

"Not a pretty picture, I'm afraid," he said, sounding as far from afraid as it was possible to be. "Loan repayments in arrears, overextended overdraft..." He shook his head and drew in his breath with a sucking sound. Jessie felt as though she's been hauled into the headmaster's study for a dressing down.

"My father died three months ago," she said. "The account was in his name."

"And now it's in yours," Vincent said, his eyes widening.

Jessie's stomach churned with irritation at this supercilious man with his 'holier than thou' attitude. "So, you're an adviser. What do you advise?"

Vincent's lips spread into a grin. "We can re-structure the loan," he said. He glanced at the figures on his screen. "We can increase the amount borrowed to cover the outstanding loan and overdraft, with interest, plus a further amount to provide working capital and service the loan, extending re-payment to..." He grinned at Jessie. "Shall we say a further three years?"

Jessie was astonished. It sounded like a most generous offer. Vincent Sowerbridge must think she'd come down in the last shower of rain. "Great," she said. "How much would I have to borrow and what would be the cost?"

"Erm." He tapped his keyboard again and stared at the screen. "Paying off the already outstanding amount, plus interest, late payment fees, arrangement fees for the new loan, interest, handling fees, administration costs, enough to tide you over until you get straight, say another six months..." He screwed up his nose and drew a piece of paper towards him. He wrote a line of figures on it and pushed it across the desk to Jessie.

Jessie's heart thumped, the air punched out of her lungs. "This much," she said, unable to believe her eyes.

"It would pay off the outstanding debt and give you enough to tide you over. It's clear that your current business is no longer viable. You need to realise your assets." He glanced at the screen again. "I see you own Watercress Farm. You'd get double that if you were to sell up under current circumstances. The bank could help with that too."

"Sell up?"

"It's an option you need to consider." He smiled, but not in a kindly way. "You know there are property developers interested in land in this area."

The self-satisfied grin on his face made Jessie's blood boil. So, just like Billy he was after the farm. "Supposing I don't want to sell up or extend my borrowing. What would happen then?"

"The bank would be forced to call in the loan. If you couldn't repay it your business would be put into Administration. Your assets would be sold, with or without your permission."

Her heart pounded. "I'll need time to think about it," she said. "It's a big step."

She could almost hear Vincent's sigh of relief as a wide grin spread across his face. "Obviously," he said. "I'll give you to the end of the month. Then come to see me again with your decision."

Jessie slunk out of that room like a whipped dog. What on earth was she going to do now?

After the site visit Luke collected his things from the hotel and checked out. He stopped at the market on his way to the station to pick up some of the speciality cheeses and fresh watercress he'd seen the previous day. He knew his friend Henri would be delighted with them.

When he arrived at the stall, he was disappointed to see a different woman serving. His heart dropped a notch or two. He recalled the vivacious girl he'd seen the day before, her laugh and the warmth of her smile.

His heart beat a little faster as he approached the stall.

"Delicious cheeses, fresh today," the lady behind the stall said with a smile. "Would you like to try some?"

"Yes please."

"Which one?"

He saw that all the cheeses had labels showing their flavour. He picked two out. She offered him samples on cocktails sticks. He tried them. They were delicious. "Do you make these yourself?" he asked.

"Yes, Drysdale Farm, that's us." She pointed to the label on the cheese.

"Hmm. I'll take one of each." He felt sure Henri would appreciate his selection. "And some watercress. Do you grow that too?"

The stallholder grinned and shook her head. "No that's our friend Jessie Tyler from Watercress Farm. But you won't get fresher."

"Jessie Tyler? Was that the girl who was here yesterday?"

"Yes, that's right, my love,"

He picked up several bunches. Watercress Farm was the farm between his father's property and the road. Billy had said it might be available to buy, which would mean the owner, the girl he saw yesterday, would be moving away. That would be a shame, he thought. If his idea for the site panned out, he'd be coming back to Netherdean, and he would have liked a chance to get to know her.

As soon as he arrived back in the office Luke uploaded the photos of the farmhouse and land they now owned and sent them to his father, along with an explanation of the multitude of difficulties they'd encounter if they tried to develop the site along the lines he envisaged. *'But I do have another idea that might be of interest,'* he wrote. *'I just need some time to flesh it out. I'll get back to you.'*

That should hold his father off for a while, he thought. Then he picked up the phone and rang Lucinda Grant, his ex-fiancée, an Events Planner and Conference Co-ordinator and invited her out to lunch.

Chapter Five

All through the drive home Jessie replayed the plans in her head. She had a lot of ideas, but she needed to detail them and produce a business plan. Once she had refined and properly costed them, she could go back to the bank and show Mr Sowerbridge that he wasn't the only one with plans for Watercress Farm. She had her own.

She wasn't stupid. She knew money would be short, but she had an idea to expand the farm and use her skills and experience to bring it back to life. She'd made plans, albeit briefly, but she'd hoped to explain them to the bank's Small Business Adviser and get his backing. Then she could work on them and make her dream of a running her own business come true.

She never got the chance. It became clear from the moment she walked into the room that Vincent Sowerbridge had ideas of his own. He was after the farm just like Billy Marks. Well, they'd both be disappointed. She'd made a promise to her father; a promise she was determined to keep.

When she arrived at the farm she saw Ned in the yard with Lady. The dog was lying down whining while Ned held his paw and seemed to be inspecting it.

"Oh no," Jessie said, rushing to his side. "What's she done?"

"Looks like she's gashed it on something," he said. "She's been gnawing it."

Jessie studied the leg Ned was holding. It was covered in blood. "It looks bad," she said. "It'll probably need a stitch. If you can get her into the truck I'll take her to the vet's to be on the safe side." She fondled the dog's ears. "We don't want it getting infected, do we, Lady?"

Ned grimaced. "Best give him a call first. If Bob's on his rounds it might be quicker for him to call rather than take her to the surgery."

"Good idea." Jessie took out her mobile phone. She'd known Bob Harris, the local vet, since her childhood. He'd been a good friend to her father for many years.

Bob answered his mobile after the first ring and said he was at a nearby farm and he'd call on Jessie as soon as he'd finished inspecting the cows.

"Meanwhile I'll disinfect it and put a bandage on," Jessie said. Her heart sank at the thought of the vet's bill after her morning at the bank, but Lady was her father's dog. She couldn't bear the thought of anything happening to her. She'd feel as though she was letting her father down.

It only took a few minutes for Jessie to get a bowl of water, add disinfectant and find a bandage.

"She'll have that off in no time," Ned said when Jessie had finished wrapping Lady's paw.

"I know." Jessie grimaced. "Still, it'll hold for a short while, until Bob arrives."

Bob Harris arrived half-an hour later. By that time Lady had almost managed to dislodge the bandage Jessie had put on, despite both Jessie and Ned trying to stop her biting at it. Jessie hadn't seen

Bob since her father's funeral. Watching him walk up the drive brought back a plethora of memories; the church service, the flowers, the kindness of the people.

She gritted her teeth and walked out to meet him.

A sturdy, well-built man in his sixties he strode up the path with a broad smile on his face. His tweed jacket had seen better days and his brown trousers, tucked into green wellington boots, also looked a little the worse for wear, but Jessie was glad to see him.

"Hi, Jessie," he said. "What's Lady been up to now?"

"Gashed her paw I'm afraid. I think she'll need a stitch and a collar."

"No problem." With Ned's help it only took him a few minutes to see to the dog. Ned went back to his work cutting the cress while Jessie made Bob a cup of coffee.

"Lady'll be right as rain in a few days," he said. "You did right to call me. Can't be too careful. She's getting on a bit, isn't she? Well, I suppose we all are."

Jessie smiled. His hair may be sparse and grey, but his eyes still twinkled.

"I've got to give you credit for keeping the farm going," he said. "It can't have been easy, but I don't suppose you'll be staying now, will you? I thought you might be of a mind to sell up now your dad's gone."

Jessie frowned. Why did everyone think she'd want to leave this place when all her memories were here?

"I don't know about that," she said. "Things are difficult, the cress doesn't pay enough to meet our expenses, but I'd hate to have to give up when my family have put so much into the farm."

"You know Holly Berry Farm's been sold to developers, don't you?" Bob said. "No-one's seen any plans yet, but there's bound to be disruption, congestion on the road, noise and dirt. Rumour is that it's to be a housing estate. There's bound to be opposition."

Jessie shrugged. She wasn't sure how she felt about the development; only that houses meant people, people meant customers. Customers meant sales and opportunities.

He shook his head. "It'd be a shame to lose the watercress beds after all these years," he said. "But I guess you can't stop progress."

"No, but you can try," she said. "Actually, I'm thinking of expanding. I've got the barns and the byres not being used. I want to turn them into riding stables. The two top fields are rented out. They'll be the paddocks. I plan to give lessons, hire out hacks, that sort of thing. I'm not going anywhere."

Bob Harris stared at her and raised his cup of coffee in a congratulatory gesture. "Well, if anyone can do it, Jessie, you can. Your dad always said you were a bright spark. Sharper than a pin, he said you were. He was right proud of you when you got that job abroad. That was something to do with horses, wasn't it?" His brow crinkled.

Another memory of Andalucía flashed through her mind. This one of Carlos and Maria brought a stab of pain. Again, she pushed it away. She'd put that particular hurt behind her and now was the time to move on. "Yes, it was a very good job. I worked with the horses in the stud. I want to do something similar here."

Bob's smile widened. "I remember your first pony, Barney, wasn't it? Great little trouper. You won all the prizes at the gymkhanas when I presented them. I always thought you had horses in your blood."

Jessie laughed. "Dad pinned all the rosettes up in my room. They're still there." A vision of her dad's face, beaming with pride when he put them on her wall, flashed into her mind. As long as she stayed at the farm she'd never forget him or Barney. Another reason to stay.

"But you'll keep the cress?"

"Oh yes. I'll never give that up," she said.

Once Bob had checked on Lady again Jessie said goodbye and went back to her father's office to work on her plans. Having spoken about them to Bob and received his obvious approval, she began with renewed enthusiasm. Sitting at her father's desk she felt the weight of her family's history staring down at her from the pictures on the walls. They seemed to be smiling down on her and offering encouragement.

She started by making a long list of what she would need to turn the existing barns and outbuildings into modern, well-equipped stables.

Dusk was falling when she heard knocking at the farmhouse door. She looked up from her papers, surprised at the gathering gloom around her. She'd been so engrossed in her plans, she'd lost track of time. She glanced at the clock. It was just past nine o'clock. Who on earth could be calling at this time of night?

The hammering became more insistent. "Okay, okay, I'm coming," she called as she rushed to open the door.

Her stomach dropped into her boots when she opened the door. Shock stole her breath.

"Buenas noches, cariño," Carlos Rodriguez said, a broad grin spread across his face. "I've been so looking forward to seeing you."

Chapter Six

It took Jessie a while to recover from the shock of seeing Carlos on her doorstep. His face was tanned, his dark hair slicked back in his usual style and laughter danced in his chocolate brown eyes. Her heart skipped a beat.

Suddenly she was back in Andalucía. She could almost feel the sun's heat creeping up her back and burning her face. Visions of the hot dusty paddocks, beautiful horses and leaning on corral fences filled her mind. The warmth and happiness of those early days, doing the best job in the world, being with people and horses she adored, it all felt so real, so close. It was as though Carlos had brought the sunshine with him even on this darkening May evening. A shiver ran through her.

Carlos laughed, put out his hand to gently lift her chin to close her gaping mouth. "Well, cariño, are you going to invite me in, or should I set up camp here on your doorstep?"

"Oh. Sorry. Come in." She stepped back to allow him to enter. Her heart thudded. She couldn't quite make sense of what her eyes were telling her. Carlos Rodriguez, here, in England. She hadn't seen him since she left Spain, so what was he doing here? What did he want?

She showed him into the kitchen. Seeing him gaze around, she saw the farmhouse kitchen through his eyes. It was very different from the luxurious hacienda his family owned. She recalled the impressive white walled building, terracotta paved terrace and extensive garden overflowing with colourful bougainvillea. Heat coloured her face. Her father had never been one for keeping up appearances. Serviceable rather than attractive, the kitchen units were dated, and the old oak table scarred from years of use. Its warmth and cosiness faded into insignificance when set again the smooth efficiency of the Rodriguez's light, airy, sun-drenched kitchen.

Although not much taller than Jessie, Carlos's presence filled the room. Suddenly the kitchen felt small, crowded and claustrophobic, or it could have been just the effect he had on her. She could hardly breathe.

"Coffee?" she said, rushing to fill the espresso machine and giving thanks that at least she'd thought to bring that home from Spain. She knew just the way he liked it.

"Gracias."

Jessie turned away from him and busied herself making the coffee. Her mind whirled. Memories of Spain ran helter-skelter though it. Memories of how close they'd been, the foolish hopes she had when he'd held her close, kissed her and whispered words of love in her ears. It had all seemed so right. Then, along came Maria with her dark liquid eyes, raven's wing hair and lilting laugh. Jessie didn't miss how Carlos cooled towards her, the hushed conversations with Maria when he thought she wasn't looking, the fluttering of her spiders' legs eye lashes. She supposed it was inevitable that Carlos would fall for sultry, fiery Maria, who came into his life like a meteor shower lighting up the night sky.

Maria came from a wealthy, old established Spanish family of landowners. What chance did Jessie, a pale faced English woman have against her heritage? Carlos and Maria; it was as though it had been written in the stars. Mary's email about her dad's illness had come at the right time. Jessie had been able to make that her excuse to come home, bury her broken heart and try to put the past behind her.

She poured the coffee. It's water under the bridge, she thought. I've moved on – but had she?

"So, cariño, this is where you grow the watercress you told me about." He grew suddenly serious. "I was sorry to hear of the loss of your father. It must have been quite a blow."

"It was." A sharp pang of memory pierced Jessie's brain.

"So now you are here all alone." The way he said it gave her goose-bumps all over. He reached out to touch her cheek. "I hoped you might contact me."

Jessie's heart pounded. She'd written to Isabella, the Rodriguez's housekeeper, but not to the family. It had all be so clear when she left. She'd come home and forget all about him. She'd make a new life for herself and he'd be a part of her distant past. "I never expected to see you again," she said.

"Really? You thought so little of me?"

"No. I… No, it's just… How's the lovely Maria?"

Carlos chuckled. "Just the same Jessie. Straight to the point, no, how do you say, no messing."

"So, how is she?"

Carlos nodded. "Maria is well. We are soon to be married." He put his cup down and looked Jessie straight in the eye. "I thought you would understand about me and Maria. It's family business. Family, heritage, continuity, that's what's important. Maria's family and mine..." He shrugged.

Jessie sighed. Of course, she understood. Family, heritage, continuity, isn't that what she wanted for the farm. To keep it going because it had kept her family for generations.

"The horses missed you," he said. "I missed you. I thought you understood about Maria."

She did understand about Maria. About how his life would be very different from hers. Men like Carlos Rodriguez married for money not love, then they took lovers as it suited them. It's what his father and his father's father had done before him. If that was what he had in mind, it wasn't a role Jessie wanted to play, not even for Carlos, despite her deep longing to be in his arms again.

"I hoped I could persuade you to come back with me, now that you have nothing to keep you here."

Jessie's eyes narrowed at his assumption. How dare he? "But I do," she said. "I have everything to keep me here. I have plans. I have a future."

He chuckled and glanced around. "This is your future, mi amor?"

"It is. It's what I want." As she said it she realised it was true. It was what she wanted more than anything; to keep the farm and to make a success of it.

Carlos shrugged. He picked up his coffee, took a sip and glanced around the kitchen again. "If you say so. But there's no reason we can't be friends is there? Very good friends?"

Jessie laughed. He was incorrigible. He never gave up. "I'll always treasure the memories of our time together," she said, "but I have a different life now."

He sighed with resignation and nodded his head. "So sad," He touched her cheek again. "I respect your honesty." He took a breath, "Perhaps now is a good time to ask for a favour?"

"A favour? Go on."

He sighed. "Horses. I have come to find horses. You were the best judge of horse flesh in the stud. We are looking to expand and for breeding stock. I was hoping to persuade you to return to Spain and help again with the horses. If you are not yet ready to do that perhaps you would help me by coming with me as I search now for stock."

Jessie's heart fluttered. Horses. Breeding stock. Wasn't that exactly what she'd been thinking about? Her plan was to turn the farm into riding stables. "It's not impossible," she said. "Finish your coffee and then I'll show you what I'm planning. We may be able to help each other."

Luke booked a table at L'huître Blanche, his ex-fiancée's favourite restaurant. If he was going to pick her brains he might as well make it as pleasant an afternoon as possible. Any time spent with Lucinda was always a joy. They'd kept in touch after an amicable separation and Luke followed her progress on social media. He'd felt a tinge of regret when he read about her engagement to Jeremy, a hedge fund manager. Regret, not envy he told himself, glad they'd managed to remain friends. He hadn't seen Lucinda since the engagement was announced but he'd sent a message of congratulations with flowers and his very best wishes.

He arrived early, determined to ensure everything was just right for the afternoon ahead. He'd mapped out his plans for development of Holly Berry Farm. This afternoon he intended to get Lucinda's opinion, and, if all went well, her support.

His heart missed a beat when she walked into the restaurant in a cloud of fragrance and possibilities. She looked stunning in her red, obviously designer, suit, her hair carefully styled and her make-up immaculate. He caught his breath. He'd forgotten how impressive she was, and today's entrance brought memories swirling in his brain.

"You look amazing, as always," he said, rising to greet her. "Being in love obviously suits you."

Lucinda laughed. "And you, Luke, are just as charming as ever." Her eyes sparkled. "Jeremy needs to look out in case I change my mind."

Luke grinned. "No danger of that," he said. "I recall how doggedly determined you could be about things once you'd made a decision."

"So, why have you invited me out if not for a trip down memory lane, and a visit to our past to tempt me away?" Her fabulous blue eyes widened.

"Which I'm sure would be a complete waste of time for us both," Luke said, although in other circumstances he could think nothing more appealing.

Lucinda smiled. "You're right of course. One should always go forward, never back."

She settled herself at the table and Luke handed her a menu. "Pleasure before business," he said. "Let's enjoy a good dinner and then I can proposition you over dessert with a clear conscience."

Lucinda's smile broadened. "I'll look forward to it." She averted her eyes to the menu but Luke didn't miss the sparkle in them.

They ordered from a young, good looking waiter wearing a white shirt under a maroon waistcoat with gold buttons. Luke ordered his usual Donegal oysters followed by beef wellington, while Lucinda went though the menu asking what each of the dishes contained. Eventually she ordered something that wasn't on the menu. "Charles knows what I like," she said. "I'm sure it'll be no problem."

The waiter smiled and Luke recalled what it was that irritated him most about Lucinda. She always had to have something different, and she wasn't happy unless she got it. No, he didn't envy

Jeremy at all. He ordered a bottle of chilled champagne which they drank while waiting for their food.

Over the meal Lucinda told Luke about her wedding plans, Jeremy's business and their planned honeymoon. Luke managed to avoid any mention of his plans until they were ready for dessert, but he couldn't help comparing the glitzy, heaving, restaurant, buzzing with hurried conversations over expensive, expense-account meals, with the rural tranquillity of Netherdean and his father's newly acquired land.

"So, I'm intrigued, Luke. Why am I here?" Lucinda asked.

Luke glanced around the restaurant. "What do you see?" he said.

Lucinda glanced around. "Mostly stressed out businessmen eating too much rich food, pumping up their blood pressure while trying to impress their clients and seal a good deal," she said. "But it's always like that here at lunch time, you should know that, Luke."

"Exactly," Luke said. "What would you think about a country retreat, surrounded by trees and fields, with state-of-the-art facilities offering businessmen a chance to enjoy rural pastimes? They could try hunting, shooting and fishing while networking, and impressing their clients to get a really great deal?"

Lucinda's brow furrowed. "Sounds like heaven. Where is this idyllic retreat and can I book it for my next conference?"

"Well, it hasn't been built yet, but I have a plan."

Lucinda chuckled. "I should have known there was a catch. So, what do you want me to do?"

"Come to my office, look over the plans, tell me what you think and, if you think it'll work, come with me to persuade my father."

Lucinda took a spoonful of her raspberry Pavlova, slid it off of her spoon into her mouth. She swallowed, fluttered her eyelashes and glared at Luke. "Sorry to be so mercenary, darling," she said, "but what's in it for me?"

Luke chuckled. Same old Lucinda he thought. "You, my darling, would be in on the ground floor of a new enterprise. Special rates for conferences, accreditation on the letterhead and a chance to build the sort of high-end, exclusive, bespoke Conference Centre you've always wanted. If we do it right, it'll be the talk of the business world and we'll make a fortune. What do you say?"

Her face lit up with a broad smile. "Sounds very appealing," she said. "Let's see the plans and I'll think about it."

Luke raised his glass. "To new beginnings and new enterprises," he said.

They clicked glasses. "New beginnings," Lucinda said. "And making a fortune."

Chapter Seven

When they'd finished their coffee Jessie took Carlos into her father's study. Dusk had fallen and she had to turn on the light. The papers spread across the mahogany desk, the worn carpet and the even more worn chair all seemed suddenly dingy as she saw them through Carlos's eyes. His father's place was always filled with sunshine, fresh and immaculately clean. She smiled. This was home to her and she wasn't going to let Carlos's presence make her feel bad, just because she hadn't had time to dust.

He glanced at the pictures on the wall. "So, these are your family?"

Jessie nodded. "My grandfather, his father and his father before him. They built the watercress farm. It's my heritage, just as the stud farm is yours."

Carlos smiled. "I see. So, no hope of you leaving here?"

"No. No hope at all," she said, smiling.

The decision was made. Seeing Carlos had brought back a tidal wave of emotion and she'd been tempted when he suggested she might return to work in Spain. Her life there would be a lot easier there than it was going to her here, where she'd struggle to keep the farm going while she built up the stables she planned. But, standing there, in the presence of her forebears, she felt the weight of family responsibility on her shoulders.

She was determined not to let them down.

She showed Carlos the papers she was working on. It was early days and she'd only sketched out a rough draft of what she aspired to achieve, but she hoped he'd be impressed.

"And you plan to breed horses here?"

"Yes. I know it's not as grand and spacious as your father's stud, but I can start small and expand."

Carlos looked doubtful.

Jessie laughed. Talking about her plans had steeled her resolve. The rented-out fields would provide the space she'd need for paddocks and a training ring. The barns and byres could be turned into stables. She could see it all in her mind's eye. "Come along," she said. "I'll show you."

She led Carlos out into the cool night air. The moon was full and a light breeze rustled the trees. Carlos walked close behind her and, for a moment, Jessie felt the warmth of his presence and memories of their months together filled her mind. She pushed them away.

They walked through the yard and out into the fields. From the top field they could see down into the valley and the amber lights from the farmhouses scattered there. Above them the sky was jewelled with stars.

"It is very beautiful," Carlos said. "I can see why you'd never want to leave this place."

He bent down and picked up a handful of grass, rubbing it between his hands. "Good pasture," he said. He sniffed the freshness of the air. "A good place. Here you will breed strong horses, cariño. I know this."

Jessie's heart swelled with pride.

As they walked the land that had been in her family for generations, Jessie told Carlos more about her plans. As well as breeding horses I can offer horses for hacking, riding lessons and pony trekking. I'm sure there'll be a market for it with the summer visitors." As she walked and talked with Carlos she knew this was where she belonged.

Inside again she made them another coffee.

"It will be a huge undertaking," Carlos said, "but if anyone can make it work it you can. I admire your spirit. It will take a great deal of money. Do you have it?"

Jessie's heart dropped several notches. She'd tried costing out her plans and had realised immediately that she'd need some sort of outside investment to carry them through. She was hoping the bank would step in, until Vincent Sowerbridge's words came to mind. Was it an impossible dream? Was she destined to fall at the first hurdle?

"I'll have to mortgage the farm," she said. Even then she wasn't sure she'd have enough.

Carlos gazed at her. "My dear, sweet Jessie," he said. "Always so full of hope and self-belief." He put his coffee cup down on the table and glanced at her again, as if in contemplation. After a few thoughtful moments he said, "If you are serious about turning this place into a stud farm you will need much help. Help I could provide if you would allow me. I have a little money of my own. I could perhaps invest." He grinned. "What do you think?"

What did she think? She thought it the most wonderful opportunity in the world. His experience and business acumen would be a great asset and she wouldn't feel so alone and overwhelmed.

A wave of deep affection for this handsome, quietly spoken man, who she'd once been so close to, washed over her. She wanted to throw her arms around him, but restrained herself, fearful of that bringing back ever more vivid memories and she didn't want to be swept back into a romance that had no future.

"A business proposition?" she said. "I'm sure we could work something out."

Suddenly the future looked a little brighter.

Luke found he enjoyed working with Lucinda. She was bright, astute and creative. She suggested keeping the farmhouse as housing for staff and building a Manor House style hotel boasting at least thirty bedrooms, a conference room, several meeting rooms, a bar and two restaurants. The outside barns would house the swimming pool and spa complex, essential for any first-class Conference and Business Centre.

Luke found his enthusiasm for the project growing. Lucinda's plans were perfect for the location. She came up with the idea of calling it The Cedars Conference and Business Centre, to evoke the image of a unique country estate and to name the suites after famous nineteenth century innovators, like Telford, Brunel and Stephenson.

"They'll inspire today's businessmen," she said. "They'll love the history of it and love the idea of being associated with yesterday's pioneering engineers and inventors."

Just as Luke had predicted, it was Lucinda's influence that persuaded his father to agree to the change in the planned development.

"It'll be amazing," she told him. "People will talk about the great time they had there. Once word spreads the sky's the limit, Mr Chambers."

Henry Chambers furrowed his brow. "Is this your idea, Luke? Do you honestly think it'll work?"

"It will, Papa," Luke said. "It's a good use of the land. We'd never get planning permission for a housing estate. There are ancient woodlands and a wildflower meadow. We'd run into all sort of conservation difficulties with anything else." He shuffled the plans on the table and laid the plan of the proposed Business Centre on top. "I've included environmentally friendly screening, and sustainable planting to preserve the landscape. This way we save the trees and meadow. It's a win/win prospect."

Henry Chambers nodded. He stroked his chin, deep in thought. Eventually he said, "If I finance it how long until we break even?"

Luke looked at Lucinda.

"I'll have no problem selling it as a prime venue," she said. "I have several clients who'll jump at the chance to spend time in the country, and they'll pay premium rates. I'd say return on investment in less than five years."

Henry's lips spread into a grin. "You always were a smart cookie, Lucinda. Can't think why this numbskull son of mine let you get away."

"Papa!"

"Oh. Okay. I'll agree to finance it on one condition. That's that you, Luke, take over the project and run it personally until we break even. You live there and manage the place until the project goes into profit. Those are my terms. Take them or leave them."

Lucinda glanced at Luke. She seemed to be willing him to say yes.

Luke's first thought was that he'd have to move out of London for the foreseeable future. The city had been the centre of his universe since he graduated from Architectural College. He wasn't sure he wanted to commit to moving away and starting life in a different place. He'd miss the glamour and excitement of living in town, the bars that buzzed with activity, the easy access to the best restaurants, theatres and exhibitions.

Then he thought of the farmhouse he'd seen, the fields stretching away over the valley, the timelessness and tranquillity of the place. It would be a challenge to make his idea work, but it was time for a new challenge and perhaps a change in his lifestyle.

A broad smile spread across his face. "It'll be my pleasure, Papa. You won't regret it. I'll make you proud."

"That's my boy," Henry said, looking suitably chuffed.

Chapter Eight

The news about the change in the development of Holly Berry Farm was soon the talk of the village. Whenever Billy met his mates in The Feathers, the talk was always about the Business and Conference Centre being built on the land. "Much better idea than a load of houses nobody wants to live in," was the general consensus. Only Billy Marks disagreed. Sitting over his pint one evening, he tried to drown the memory of the commission he'd lose with the loss of the housing development.

"I never reckoned they'd get permission for a housing development, anyway," someone said, "but won't a Conference Centre take trade away from the hotel? We get a lot of summer visitors. How will they be affected?"

"They won't. It'll be businessmen in sharp suits and shiny shoes. They won't want to venture into town."

"The Business Centre will bring money into the town and revive it," Dennis, the builder said. "We're already benefitting and so will everyone else when it opens. They'll want local produce and they'll employ local staff, so it's a win/win all round."

Billy wasn't convinced.

"You never know," Dennis said. "If them businessmen like the look of the place they might be after buying their own properties here. That'll mean a good commission."

Billy sighed. "I'll not be holding my breath," he said. Still, he thought, surely a Business Centre would need better access than the dirt road to Holly Berry Farm allowed? Jessie had been annoyed at his suggestion, but once she had time to think and the reality of her situation hit her, he was sure he could persuade her to sell Watercress Farm. After all, there was nothing to keep her here, was there?

Carlos insisted upon seeing her accounts and when he saw the size of the debts outstanding he agreed to advance enough to repay them, plus set her up with a couple of breeding mares.

"You need to start with a clean sheet," he said. "Don't let the debts of the past weigh you down. If we are going into business together, we need to see a clear way ahead."

Jessie nodded, her heart filled with gratitude. At least now she'd have no need to worry about the bank foreclosing. The vision of Vincent Sowerbridge's face flashed through her mind. She'd enjoy taking him down a peg or two.

Carlos grinned and his eyes twinkled as he said. "I intend to take a personal interest in our business together."

Once the papers were signed and she had Carlos's cheque in her hand, she visited the bank for another meeting with Vincent Sowerbridge. When she produced the funds to clear her outstanding debt, his demeanour changed from hostile to quite obsequious.

"These Spanish investors," he said. "Can you arrange an introduction?"

Jessie laughed. But he did agree to her request for a business loan to cover the cost of the rebuilding and renovations she would need.

Her next port of call was the local builders' yard where the owner, Dennis Hayes, and his son, Jim, greeted her. When she showed them her plans for the new stables Dennis nodded. "We're supplying materials for the development of the old Cosby farm. That's out your way isn't it? Should be easy to fit this in with what we're doing there."

"I heard it was being developed," she said. "A housing estate isn't it?"

Dennis shook his head. "No. It's a big house they're going to turn into a Conference Centre for businessmen," he said. "Swimming pool, spa, the lot. Apparently them townies will pay the earth for a chance to meet up and try some rural pursuits."

"What like digging potatoes and milking cows?" Jim asked, looking bewildered.

"Nah, you knucklehead. They mean shooting and fishing. Least that's what I heard."

Jessie smothered her mirth at the vision of men in suit digging potatoes or milking cows as Jim had suggested.

"Not much fishing up at old Cosby's place," Jim said.

"Oh they got plans for that, and clay pigeon for the shooting. I doubt they'll have pheasant. Too much work."

"It sounds like a big job, you'll be kept busy then."

"Nah, not us. They've got their own construction company, but we're supplying the local materials, and some of the extra labour, so good news all round I reckon."

As Jessie left the yard she couldn't help thinking about the opportunities for her business the new development of Holly Berry Farm would bring. Rural pursuits must include riding, surely?

One of the conditions of her new business partnership was that she would travel the country with Carlos looking for suitable horses, both for her stables and for his father's stud. Carlos had also persuaded his father to leave any mares they bought in their newly built stables, instead of transporting them home.

"You have good pasture," Carlos said. "He knows they'll be in good hands and he'll pay a generous fee."

His father also agreed to provide an experienced stable hand to manage the renovations while Jessie was away.

Miguel, a well built, swarthy, taciturn man in his early forties, arrived before they left. Jessie remembered him. He was experienced and reliable. She knew she could trust him and any worries she'd had about leaving melted away.

She left Ned in charge of the farm. Mary or Tom would call each day to pick up the cress for the market and make sure everything at the farm was going ahead as planned. She took on a local lad from the village to work with Ned and help in the watercress beds planting out the new season's cress.

Miguel would be in charge of the renovation of the stables. Dennis Hayes promised that the work would be finished by the time Jessie returned from her buying trip with Carlos.

The two weeks horse hunting with Carlos flew. Jessie had forgotten what good company he was and she loved working with the horses again. She hadn't realised how much she missed the atmosphere of a working stud and the smell of manure and rotting hay that permeated the air in the yards they visited.

She also hadn't realised how difficult it would be spending so much time with Carlos. She'd forgotten how he made her laugh, how attentive he was to her needs and how he made her feel special. Every day problems melted away and she felt closer to him. It was only the memory of Maria waiting at home for him that kept her to her resolve not to get involved with him again. Still, it didn't stop her enjoying his company, relishing the scent of him, the warmth of his smile and the closeness of him, did it?

By the time they returned to Watercress Farm the stables were complete and, with the horses she'd bought, she was almost ready to open her new business.

Miguel was staying on and would take on the responsibility of the breeding mares, his speciality. Jessie would have her hands full with the riding hires, hacking and pony trekking together with the paperwork, which she didn't relish. She also had a feeling that Miguel, although he didn't say much, noticed everything and would report back to Senor Rodriguez.

She felt a tinge of sorrow when Carlos left.

"Don't worry, cariño, I will be back again soon." He kissed her cheek and the familiar thrill ran through her. She chided herself for her susceptibility.

"Remember me to Maria," she said as she waved him goodbye. "Good luck with the wedding. May all your troubles be little ones." Carlos made no secret of his desire for a large family. That was one thing she didn't envy – not now she had her own business to run and was able to combine her passion for horses with her family's heritage.

Over the next few weeks, she got her licence, took on more staff and spent her evenings looking for tack, helmets and hay. She had leaflets and brochures printed. She worked from dawn to dusk getting everything ready, while Miguel looked after the horses.

Chapter Nine

As soon as the plans for the Business Centre had been finalised and planning permission granted, Luke drove Lucinda to Netherdean to see the site at the centre of their plans.

His father had sent a construction team ahead to start laying the foundations and by the time Luke and Lucinda arrived Holly Berry Farm resembled a building site. Luke burned with excitement, but the visit didn't go well. As soon as Lucinda stepped out of the car she caught her red stiletto heel in a muddy rut, turning her ankle. Luke had to carry her into farmhouse kitchen to look at the injury. It wasn't as bad as he feared and she was soon on her feet again, but the experience hadn't endeared the place to her.

"Not the most sensible shoes to wear to a construction site," he said.

Lucinda pouted. When she stepped back outside a million midges swarmed around her head. "Honestly, Luke, you might have warned me," she said, batting them away.

"It's probably your perfume's exotic undertones," he told her.

Lucinda grimaced and glanced around. "Exotic undertones? Completely lost in the open air. No, it's the countryside. Only bearable if gazed at through a window, accompanied by good food and a glass of bubbly. I can see the potential of the location," she said, "but I think I'll come back when it's finished. We can have a Grand Opening. I'll invite everyone who's anyone. I can see it now, oysters and champagne on the terrace – then the countryside's just about bearable."

Luke laughed but drove her back into town. On the way he took her around all the areas of historical interest, pointing them out, so they could be included in the brochures she was preparing. Then, after lunch in The Feathers, which Lucinda declared was 'quite quaint', Luke put her on the train back to London.

Soon the track to Holly Berry Farm was filled with a succession of trucks and lorries carrying building materials up to the site. Sand and dust filled the air. Over the weeks Jessie watched the transformation from a run-down, dilapidated farm to a magnificent Manor House complete with outbuildings housing a swimming pool and spa, landscaped gardens and a lake built alongside the existing forestry and wildflower meadow.

By August the new stables were up and running to her satisfaction and, to her surprise, Carlos returned.

"I have to keep an eye on my investment," he said, the familiar gleam in his dark eyes. Jessie thought it was more than that, but she welcomed his experience.

With him and Miguel looking after the stud side of the business she prepared herself to approach the Business Centre to offer her services. She hoped they would be the first customers for her new venture. She made extensive enquiries about the developers responsible for the Centre. She found out the name of the man in charge. She didn't want to be passed from pillar to post and get nowhere so she telephoned his secretary and made an appointment. She didn't want a wasted journey either.

That night she honed her pitch. She'd take some fresh cress for tasting, a dossier of information giving details of the fifteen vitamins and minerals it contained and a list of reasons why it should feature on their menu. She even included one or two of her mother's favourite watercress recipes along with a list of the specialist cheeses Tom and Mary could supply. Then she added several brochures outlining the 'Equestrian Experience' she was going to offer. Once she'd got all her materials together she ran through her spiel. It was an anxious time. This pitch could make all the difference to the success or otherwise of her new business. She didn't want to fall at the first hurdle, it was too important to her.

The next morning butterflies ricocheted in her stomach. She thought of the photos lining the walls of her father's study. Six generations had farmed the land before her. She was determined not to be the last of the line or to fail through not matching up to the moment.

The Business Centre stood at the end of a long driveway. If it hadn't been for the scaffolding and the plethora of builders' equipment, Jessie would have sworn she was approaching a centuries-old Manor House.

She parked in front of a portacabin. A notice proclaimed it to be '*The Office of the CEO of the Cedars Conference and Business Centre.*'

She took a breath and gathered up her papers. This was her chance to show everyone what she was made of. She got out of her ancient Land Rover, walked over and knocked on the door.

A tall, good-looking man in faded blue jeans and open-necked shirt opened the door. He had a curly mop of tousled dark hair and the bluest eyes Jessie had ever seen. Her heart jolted when she saw him. His smile broadened when he saw her.

"Hi," he said. "Come in. I'm Luke Chambers, CEO of the Cedars Conference and Business Centre."

Jessie stepped into the office, her heart racing. It was cool and bright. A desk with a telephone and computer stood in the middle of the room. Two chairs and three filing cabinets were the only other pieces of furniture. A line of framed certificates graced the wall and she wasn't surprised to see Rugby and Cricket team photos hanging alongside them. His athletic build suggested a love of sports.

"It's Jessie Tyler from Watercress Farm isn't it?" he said. "I've seen you in the market. We're neighbours. I meant to call on you. Billy Marks, the estate agent, said you were thinking of selling up."

So, he was one jump ahead of her. He already knew who she was. She recalled Mary telling her about a man who'd asked after her the day she went to the bank. Luke Chambers fitted Mary's description exactly. Of course she hadn't realised he was the developer who was after her land. She was thrilled he'd noticed her, but she wasn't going to get involved with a man who, according to Billy Marks, wanted to tear up the watercress beds for a car park. "I'm sorry to disappoint you," she said. "I have no intention of selling Watercress Farm."

He grinned. "I'm not disappointed," he said. "I was hoping that wasn't the case. I'll be looking to source locally grown produce and your watercress and speciality cheeses would sit well on our menus. I'm delighted to hear you're staying. I hope we will be good friends as well as neighbours."

"I hope so too," Jessie said and found, to her great relief, she really meant it. "I can offer you cress, cheese and something more."

His eyebrows rose. A glint of humour lit up his swimming pool eyes.

She smiled and took out her Equestrian Experience brochures. "I run a riding stable and can offer your clients the chance to ride one of our magnificent horses through some of England's most beautiful countryside."

His smile broadened. He took the leaflet she offered. "Equestrian Experience? I can see our clients being thrilled with that, but I'd have to try it out myself before I could recommend it."

"No problem," she said. "Have you ridden before?"

"Does riding a donkey across the Himalayan foothills count?"

She laughed. "I think we can do better than a donkey," she said. "I'm sure you'll pick it up in no time."

Excitement fizzed through her, but Jessie was brought down to earth when the door opened and a woman in five inch heels and, what Jessie guessed was a very expensive suit, burst in.

"Luke, darling," she said, ignoring Jessie who sat open mouthed staring at her. "I need you to rescue me and take me out to a super indulgent lunch to restore my equilibrium." She glanced at Jessie as though seeing her for the first time.

"Lucy, this is Miss Tyler. She's come to offer us watercress and horses."

Lucinda wrinkled her nose. "Horses? Big smelly brutes. Why do we want horses?"

"Not us. The clients. She's offering an Equestrian Experience. I think it will go down rather well. What do you think?" He handed her Jessie's leaflet.

Lucinda shrugged and passed the leaflet back. "Darling, I'm incapable of thought until I've had a decent lunch, if such a thing exists in this god-forsaken place."

Luke laughed. "Okay, lunch it is." He turned to Jessie, "Thank you for coming, Miss Tyler. I think horses are a wonderful idea. We're not quite up and running yet, but when we are I'll be in touch."

Jessie shook the hand he extended towards her. "Thank you," she managed to mutter. She turned to the interruption. "I hope you enjoy your lunch. I think you'll find the hotel does a pretty good spread." She opened the door to leave. "Worth a try anyway."

Outside she stopped and took a breath. Her heart pounded. Had she been too bold? Would they think her rude? A country bumpkin who didn't know any better? She wasn't sure whether it was irritation at the woman who'd barged in, or delight at the possibility of Mr Luke Chambers coming to try out one of her horses, that bothered her most. Who was that woman anyway? Were they a couple? Neither wore wedding rings, she'd noticed that, but the woman had a rock the size of a pebble on her engagement finger. Jessie's heart sunk a little.

He'd seemed interested in her proposition, or was he just being polite? Suddenly what he thought seemed important. Thanks to Carlos, and his father stabling fees, her business would survive whether they took up her offer or not. So, why did Mr Luke Chambers' opinion matter so much?

Chapter Ten

After seeing Lucinda off on the train back to town Luke called into The Feathers for a drink. He'd picked up the local paper and wanted to see if there was anything in it about the Business Centre and its development. His clients would judge their experience by how they were treated from the moment they stepped down from the train. They needed to feel welcome, so the opinions of the locals would be vital to his success. He'd heard how everyone knew everybody else's business in close knit communities, but had never witnessed it until he came to Netherdean. Nor did he realise how avidly they followed their neighbours' progress. He didn't get involved any more than he had to, being an outsider, but, as he'd be living there, he did his best to blend in, while not actively taking part in it.

As he sat reading a group of men from the market came in. He couldn't help but overhear their conversation.

"I see Billy Marks has got is knickers in a twist," he heard one say. "Didn't have two good words to say to me this morning. What's rattled his cage?"

"Jessie Tyler's given 'im the elbow," came the response.

Luke's ears pricked up at the mention of Jessie Tyler's name. His heart had lifted when she'd come into his office with her brochures and recipes. He remembered her from the market and the impression she'd made then. Seeing her again, his view of her hadn't changed, if anything he'd grown more intrigued. "'E was hoping to get 'is feet under the table there and get his hands on the farm but she's got her fancy man from Spain come over. 'E'll be running the place now."

Luke put his paper down and listened more intently.

"I heard she'd paid off old man Tyler's debts," the first one said. "Must be worth a bit, 'er fancy man."

"Wealthy family, I heard. Now the old man's gone she's making hay. Can't blame 'er can you?"

The men commiserated with Billy in his absence and the conversation turned to the day's trade and the possibility of rain before dark.

A worm of worry turned in Luke's stomach, but he didn't know why. His heart dropped a little, but he thought he shouldn't be surprised. She was an attractive girl. He'd be surprised if she didn't have lots of admirers. In any case, what Miss Tyler did was none of his business and he wasn't one to listen to village gossip as a rule, but the mention of a man taking over her farm, and presumably a lot more than that, intrigued him. When he'd first arrived, Billy Marks had suggested that Watercress Farm might be up for sale, but Miss Tyler herself had told him she wasn't going anywhere. Obviously, the intervention of the man they were talking about was what had made the difference. He decided he wanted to know more about this man and his intentions. Only as far as it might affect the Business Centre, he told himself. Nothing to do with anything else.

He folded his newspaper and left the pub more ill at ease than when he'd arrived.

Back at the stables Jessie couldn't get Luke Chambers out of her mind. They were obviously a couple, him and that 'interruption', but she wasn't sure why that should disturb her. Only because he'd be leaving to go back to town she told herself. There was no way Madam would stay. If he left she'd have to deal with someone else if she wanted to do business with them. That was why she was so concerned, nothing else.

Later that afternoon she went to talk to her neighbour, Mary. She had to collect what was left of the cress, any that hadn't sold, which would go to the processing plant. Mary always knew what was going on in Netherdean, so Jessie looked forward to a good old gossip.

After hearing all the news from the market, the local's views of the Business Centre came up.

"It's an opportunity, for sure," Mary said. "I hear they're planning a grand opening."

Jessie smiled, you couldn't keep much quiet in Netherdean.

"According to Mrs Thornbury, that woman's arranging it, you know, high heels and a face like a painted peach. Probably spends more on having her hair done than I spend on a week's dinners. If she's in charge it'll be costing a fortune. We could all do with a bit of that."

Jessie's heart tumbled. Mrs Thornbury had been taken on as a cleaner and not much got past her.

She'd know more about what was going on up there than anyone. "What does Mrs Thornbury think will happen after the opening?" Jessie asked. "Will Mr Chambers stay on?"

Mary put her mixing bowl down and stared at Jessie. "Luke Chambers? Got a soft spot 'ave you? I'm not surprised. He'd be quite a catch. I thought he was interested in you too.

Jessie's eyebrows rose. Interested in her? Some hope, the thought, but she couldn't deny the attraction and the excitement that fizzed through her whenever she thought of him. "I believe he's already spoken for," she said.

Mary shrugged her shoulders. "Hmm, yes. I suppose that painted doll is more his speed." She returned to her mixing bowl. "What about that chap you've got at the farm? I thought you and 'im…"

"Well, you thought wrong. He's a business partner, that's all."

Mary chuckled. "If you say so."

Jessie couldn't help but smile. Once upon a time she'd had high hopes of Carlos, but they'd been dashed. Her heart had been bruised, if not quite broken. Was she setting up false hopes again hankering after a man she couldn't have? Perhaps it would be best if Mr Luke Chambers went away. She decided then to stay well away from him and his Business Centre.

Chapter Eleven

By the end of the week Luke was happy with the progress of the building work and decided, it being a clear autumnal morning, to take up Jessie's offer of a ride out, especially as it meant a chance to see her again. It had been a while since he'd been on a horse, but considered himself a competent horseman, if a little rusty. His quip about riding a donkey across the Himalayas had been made to put Jessie at her ease. He'd ridden widely in his travels across Europe. But there was no need for her to know that.

He telephoned to book an hour's appointment, explaining to the stable hand, who spoke little English, that he hadn't been on a horse for a while, so that should be taken into consideration when choosing a mount for him. According to the brochure riding hats and other suitable gear would be provided.

That afternoon he walked down the hill to the stables, a buzz of anticipation humming through him. He assured himself that it was the thought of being on a horse again that made him so nervous, not seeing Jessie Tyler.

A light breeze rustled the trees as he walked towards the farm. A squirrel darted out in front of him and dashed up a tree. He saw a rabbit on the grassy verge. He smiled at it and it disappeared into the hedgerow. When he reached the farm he saw an elderly man and a lad up to their knees in the stream that ran through the property. The famous watercress, he thought, admiring its glossy greenness. A Labrador curled up in front of the farmhouse door raised its head, sniffed the air as he passed, but didn't get up. He gazed at the farmhouse where Jessie Tyler lived. It looked old and settled. He imagined a cosy kitchen with copper pans and an old oak table, and front room with a blazing fire. He chided himself for letting his imagination run away with him.

The stable yard was a different matter. New modern buildings surrounded an area being swept by a young lad. The unmistakable smell of hay and horse manure hung in the air and he heard the skittering and shuffling of the animals in their boxes. It all looked very smart and busy with a pervasive atmosphere of purpose.

He guessed it was the stable hand he'd spoken to earlier who greeted him when he arrived.

"Is Miss Tyler around?" he asked. "I wanted to speak to her about the sort of service the stables could provide."

The stable hand shook his head. "Senor Rodriguez is here."

Luke's heart sank, but sure enough, as they were speaking Carlos Rodriguez appeared. "Ah, Mr Chambers," he said, holding out his hand. "I heard you were coming. I'm sure we can fit you up with a great ride." He turned to the stable hand. "Miguel, get Star ready for Mr Chambers. I'll take Warrior." He smiled. "Star is a great horse, you'll like him."

"I was hoping to see Miss Tyler."

"She'll be sorry to miss you, but she should be back soon. Some problem with the farm, the cress, something she had to sign." He shrugged. "Shall we?" He pointed to the tack room and Luke followed him in. Once he'd been fitted with a hat and boots he strode out, still hoping to see Jessie but instead he saw Miguel lead out two horses, saddled and ready to go. They looked much bigger than he remembered. One was black with a white star on his forehead and white socks on each of his legs. The other was chestnut and far less forbidding. The black horse, which he rightly guessed was Star, tossed his head, impatient to be off. Luke swallowed.

Before he could make a move, Jessie Tyler drove into the yard. Her eyes widened when she saw the horses and Luke Chambers ready to mount up.

"What are you doing, Carlos?" A trill of alarm heightened her voice. "Mr Chambers is a novice. I told Miguel to get Blackberry ready for him. Star is much too highly strung." She grabbed Star's bridle.

"Cariño," Carlos greeted her. "I'm afraid Blackberry has a slight limp. I noticed it this morning. We are waiting for the vet to call. I'm sure Mr Chambers would prefer a proper horse." He grinned at Luke.

"Blackberry was fine this morning when I took her feed."

Carlos swung himself into the saddle of the chestnut horse. The horse whinnied and reared, sending a cloud of vapour into the air, stamping its feet as Carlos reined it in. "Come Mr Chambers, let us blow the cobwebs away."

Luke knew he'd been set up, but it felt like a challenge and excitement coursed through his veins. This man obviously thought he could get the best of him, but why? He clearly had some claim to the stables and Jessie Tyler too, but why should he see Luke as an adversary? Perhaps he felt threatened by his presence? Luke hoped so. "Great," he said, climbing onto the mounting block. "What do I do now?"

Carlos laughed. Miguel took the bridle from Jessie and helped Luke into the saddle. Eventually they managed to ride out, both horses champing at the bit ready to go, leaving Jessie staring after them, a look like thunder on her face.

Watching them ride away anger and irritation swirled inside Jessie. She'd told Miguel to saddle up Blackberry for Mr Chambers, now Carlos had over-ridden her instructions and had Star, a hard to handle hunter, saddled up instead. What was he trying to prove? That he was a better horseman than a man from the city who'd rarely, if ever, sat astride a horse? If Blackberry was limp there were other hacks he could have chosen. Chevron and Topper were both more docile and easier rides. What was Carlos thinking of?

Her heart pounded as she led Blackberry out of her stable. Gingerly she checked each of her legs. She led her around the yard. She saw no sign of a limp.

"Miguel, did Blackberry have a limp this morning? She looks alright to me."

Miguel shrugged. She sighed with fury and frustration. It was good of Senor Rodriguez to send his top hand to oversee the building of the stables and she was aware that everything that went on there was reported back to him. He was taking care of his son's investment. She couldn't blame him for that, but she'd never envisaged Carlos being so hands-on in the running of the place. His interference was beginning to infuriate her.

Of course, it was a way to keep her close, why wouldn't he want that? He'd made it clear that his engagement need not change their relationship. It was Jessie who insisted on coming home, but what he did was stupid and reckless. If Star bolted or threw his rider she could lose her licence and her business with it. She'd have to have it out with Carlos. It was all very well him feeding his ego by showing up the man who could possibly be her best client. If anything happened to Luke Chambers because of Carlos's brainless macho pride she'd never forgive him.

Leading Blackberry back into her stable she pushed down her irritation. She hadn't wanted to make a fuss in front of Luke, but Carlos's behaviour rankled. Carlos was Carlos. She knew what he was like, and she couldn't afford to upset him. She recalled how desperately she'd needed his help. If it hadn't been for him she'd have nothing. The farm would be gone and she'd have had to find a job working for someone else. She knew she should be grateful, but the gratitude didn't come easily, especially since he'd broken her heart, and was now intent on wrecking her business.

Sitting astride Star as he walked him out of the gate behind Carlos Rodriguez, Luke gazed around. He'd forgotten how high up and far from the ground he'd be. Also, the horse was wider than he remembered and more difficult to control. Carlos nudged Warrior into a trot and Star followed suit to keep abreast of them. It took Luke a while to get into the rhythm of the ride, feeling the horse beneath him, adjusting his seat to its pace. They trotted along a bridle path. The afternoon sunlight dappled around them, glowing through the trees, a tapestry of red, gold and orange. The earthy smell of damp grass and wood scented the air. It was very different from being in the city Luke thought. A real pleasure to be out. He began to see the benefits to living in the countryside.

When they came to open fields Carlos nudged Warrior into a canter and Star followed. Luke soon adjusted to the new rhythm. His instincts served him well. A great sense of freedom filled him as the horse's pace quickened and the rhythmic pounding of hooves on turf rang in his ears. He sensed rather than saw the open fields around them as they passed, the cool clean air bringing a glow to his cheeks. After about ten minutes, Carlos reined his horse in. "Race you to the copse," he said.

Luke gazed ahead to a stand of trees about half a mile away. Before Luke had a chance to answer, Carlos was off at a gallop. Star, obviously used to the race, took to his heels after Warrior. If it hadn't been for Luke pressing his knees as hard as he could into the horse's side he would have fallen. As it was, he leaned into the ride, holding the horse back with the reins until he was ready. Then he gave Star his head and they were off across the meadow. The exhilaration was new to Luke. He thrilled at the power of the beast beneath him as they thundered across the meadow, the cool air whistling by, relishing the sheer excitement of being astride such a mount. The ride seemed endless. Star swerved to a halt as they reached the copse. Again Luke almost lost his seat, but just managed to hang on. "Phew!" he said. "That was quite a ride."

Carlos laughed. "That was nothing. One day we will have a real race, yes?"

"Thank you," Luke said. "But I'm not sure that was quite what Miss Tyler had in mind for my clients. They will have had less experience than I and may not fare as well."

Carlos laughed again. "For real riding you have to come to Espana. But for your clients, we have hacks." To Luke's ears, he sounded quite dismissive. Again Luke wondered about his and Jessie's relationship.

Back at the stable relief flooded over Jessie when she saw them riding home, both looking pleased with themselves. Mr Chambers had obviously shown himself to be equal to the challenge that Star presented to any new rider. She was glad. Anything that put a dent in Carlos's arrogant pride was okay with her. Then she chided herself for her unkind thoughts. Anything Carlos did these days seemed to rub her up the wrong way. The memory of Maria announcing their engagement filled her mind and she had to swallow back the bitter resentment rising inside her.

"How was it?" she said grabbing Star's bridle. "He's a lovely horse, I hope he treated you well."

"An amazing ride," Luke said, sliding down from the saddle. He grinned and rubbed his back. "Which I'm sure, I'll pay for tomorrow morning."

Jessie smiled, reassured. It was going to be okay. At least he wasn't angry or upset, although he had every right to be furious with them. She was still furious with Carlos.

"It's not quite what I had in mind for our clientele," he said, still rubbing his back.

"No." Jessie glared at Carlos, who'd dismounted and was leading Warrior away to be rubbed down. He waved at her, a broad grin on his face and her heart flipped. So annoying that he still had that effect on her, she thought.

"We have other horses, but my partner wanted you to experience the best," she said in his defence. "I hope it hasn't put you off."

"No. On the contrary. I'd like to do it again and I feel sure that, together, we can offer my clients something really special." Jessie saw a mischievous glint in his eye as he said it. She also didn't miss the emphasis on the word, together. She smiled as warmth flowed through her. Perhaps Carlos had something to worry about after all.

She thought she'd handled that quite well, considering the anger that still writhed inside her. Once Luke had gone she went to confront Carlos.

"What on earth do you think you were doing? Putting a novice on Star. Have you any idea what could have happened? If he'd been thrown or fallen it would ruin any chance of getting the Centre's business. In fact a bad fall could ruin my business all together."

"Your business? You mean OUR business." A dark shadow crossed Carlos's face. Jessie shivered with anxiety. She'd seen that look before. It was usually followed by an outburst of fury that left better men than her shaking. She stared at him but his temper disappeared in an instant. He shrugged. "They are chaff in the wind – soon gone." He touched her face. "You and I, cariño, we will build good stud together. The hacking, the riding lessons – puff – they are of no consequence." He leaned towards her, his lips brushed her cheek before he turned and walked away.

Jessie boiled inside. This wasn't the way it was supposed to be. He'd become quite overbearing. She'd always put his temper down to passion and his fiery Latin blood, but today it looked more like petulant perverseness. There was no getting away from it; she'd seen a different side of him when he didn't get his own way. Then she remembered: in Spain he always got his own way.

Chapter Twelve

Later that evening Jessie heard from Mary that Tom had sprained his ankle and wouldn't be able to man the stall the next day. It being Saturday, the busiest day in the market, could Jessie fill in? "Of course," she said. I hope Tom's okay."

"It's just a sprain," Mary said. "He should be fine in a couple of days, but he does need to rest it."

The next morning Jessie rose early and made breakfast. Lady greeted her, as always, nuzzling up to her. Jessie stroked the old dog's head. "You okay?" she whispered, ruffling her ears. "I don't suppose you want to wander out much today either. There'll be a cold wind and it looks like rain." As she said it she thought of her day ahead. The weather wouldn't deter the customers. She'd have to get a move on if she wanted to be set up before people started wandering in. She sighed. The only bookings for the stables were lessons for the local children, which Sally, the girls from the village who helped out at weekends, could easily manage. She fed Lady and made herself some sandwiches and coffee to take with her. She finished her breakfast and had another cup of coffee while she waited for Ned to arrive to let him know where she'd be.

"I'll be needing to get the sheeting out," he said. "Weather's turning colder."

Jessie nodded. Over winter the cress would have to be protected from frost and new plantings set out for the coming year. Between Ned and the lad she'd taken on they should be able to manage it. She was well aware of the extra work that went into producing the cress over the colder seasons, and that the money it brought in didn't really cover the cost. Still, watercress was her family's heritage. She couldn't give up on it. "If there's anything else you need, any extra sheeting, straw, anything, just let me know."

Ned nodded.

Once she'd checked that everything was in order at the stables she drove out to pick up the cheeses from Mary and then made her way into town. She usually enjoyed market days. She liked the people who thronged around, their friendly, smiling faces. Despite the chill in the air, she'd enjoy the day.

She took her time setting the stall up, laying the cheeses out just as Mary liked them. A brisk wind flapped the awnings and she tightened the ropes that held the canvas. While she was setting up the memory of the previous day ran through her mind. She was still mad at Carlos. His recklessness could have wrecked any chance she had of doing business with Mr Chambers. Luckily he'd taken it in his stride and she had to admire his cool-headed tenacity. If he'd had a fall they'd have been in real trouble. Not only the loss of business, but he could probably sue them if he'd been injured. The more she thought about it, the crosser she became with Carlos. Clearly their ideas for the future of the business clashed. That was a hurdle she'd have to overcome.

Around mid morning she glanced up to see Billy Marks standing looking over the stall. He looked a lot more worn and wearier than the last time she'd seen him. "Morning, Billy," she said. "What can we do for you today?"

Billly shrugged. "It's been a while, Jessie. Just thought I'd see how you were."

The memory of their last meeting fizzed through Jessie's mind. She'd managed to get back on her feet and hang onto the farm. She supposed she should forgive him. He was just taking care of his business the same as she was thinking about hers. "Well, I'm fine, as you can see," she said. "Still surviving. How about you?"

He chuckled, but not with mirth. "We don't all have rich boyfriends who can bail us out." He shook his head. "Sorry Jess. That didn't come out the way I meant."

Jessie thought it had come out exactly the way he meant, but she felt sorry for him. It can't have been easy taking on his father's business, especially when his father had left it in such a state. "It's okay, Billy," she said. "I know we've had our run-ins but it's all in the past. Life goes on."

He smiled and his face brightened. He's not so bad looking when he smiles, Jessie thought.

"Well, don't forget, if ever you want to sell up…"

"You'll be the first to know," Jessie said with a grin.

"Thanks, Jess. You're a star."

By mid-afternoon Jessie was thinking of packing up. The earlier crowds had thinned and the sky clouded over, threatening rain. Trade had been brisk and the cash box full enough to have made it worthwhile opening up the stall. There were some cheeses left and a little cress. She started to put the cheeses back into the freezer boxes when she heard a voice. "I'm not too late, am I?"

She glanced around. Luke Chambers stood in front of her, a worried look on his face. "I'd hoped to pick up some cheese and some of your fresh cress to take with me. My friend in London loves it."

"Oh." Jessie didn't know what to say. She noticed he was wearing his business suit and carried a briefcase. "You're just in time," she said. "What would you like?"

His eyes sparkled. "Well now, there's a question. Let me see."

Jessie got the impression that it was more than cheeses he was after, and she found she didn't mind a bit. "Will you be gone long?" The question slipped from her brain to her mouth and out before she could stop it. "I mean…erm…"

He laughed and the air between them seemed to evaporate, all chill gone. "My ex-fiancée is planning a grand opening for the Business Centre. I have to go to town to make all the arrangements. I expect to be gone for a week. Perhaps when I return I could take one of your horses out again?"

Covered in confusion and all fingers and thumbs, Jessie put some cheeses and cress into a bag, not at all sure what she was doing. Ex-fiancée. He said ex-fiancée. "Yes. That would be lovely," she stammered, her stomach churning.

"Great," he said, taking the bag she offered and handing her a ten-pound note. "I look forward to it."

Then he was gone and Jessie was left wondering why her heart was all aflutter. Ex-fiancée, she thought and for some reason the day seemed brighter.

On the train Luke worked on plans for the grand opening. The week ahead was filled with meetings, the first and most intimidating, being with his father. He'd kept him abreast of progress, but the old man had never visited the site and Luke found it impossible to convey the incalculable beauty of the environment and the magic of the countryside to a man who thought only in pounds, shillings and pence. Luke thought back to all they'd achieved. When he'd first arrived in Netherdean spring sunshine filled the air, bluebells carpeted woods and trees showed their first buds of new life. He'd felt a tranquillity that had never left him. There were no words to describe how he'd felt when he moved from the hotel into the caravan on site: the impenetrable darkness of the night, the silence, punctuated by the hooting of owls or the scurry and scratching of mice outside. The whistle of the wind through the trees. The beauty of the dawn. All these things he'd come to appreciate, things he could never explain to his father.

He'd become involved in all aspect of the project from the renovation and expansion of the farmhouse to provide staff quarters, to the building of the Manor House, Conference Centre and Spa. He counted the milestones in his head: getting the plans accepted, laying the first stones, seeing it develop before his eyes. He hoped his father would be impressed. Now autumn's rich tapestry, golden corn, rape and linseed coloured the fields and it was time to reap the harvest of his efforts.

There were a few problems to be ironed out, but over all, Luke felt a sense of pride. On time and under budget. That would be his father's measure of success, but for Luke it was the involvement of the local community, being part of something much bigger and providing a lasting legacy, that's what inspired him.

The Business Centre, when it opened, would provide employment, and increased trade for the town. Transport still bothered him. The train to Netherdean was slow and ponderous. Would providing a bus from the Main Line Station be better? A fleet of limousines was a possibility but that would be prohibitively expensive and probably underused. For VIPs they could possibly hire a helicopter, that would go down well, but the cost would be outrageous. Still, outrageous was often good for business. People liked being spoiled outrageously, and cosseted to within an inch of asphyxiation.

As he pondered the alternatives he glanced from time to time out of the window at the passing scenery. The memory of galloping across fields filled his mind, the sights, sounds and smells fresh and clear. Then there was Jessie, her face always fresh and clear in his mind too. She appeared good and wholesome. He chuckled to himself at the memory of her face as he mounted Star, a picture of shocked alarm, which, when he returned intact, turned to surprise mixed with relief and, he hoped, not a little admiration. Her relief was tiny compared to his. He felt he'd been put to the test and, more by luck than judgement, sailed through. Again he chuckled to himself. Then he remembered Carlos and sighed with resignation. She was spoken for. No use getting your hopes up there old lad, he said to himself. She's taken, more's the pity.

Chapter Thirteen

The next morning Jessie was surprised to see Carlos arrive in a taxi, wearing a suit, rather than the casual jeans or jodhpurs he wore around the stables. Her heart fluttered. He looks even more handsome, she thought as he came towards her. A deep frown creased his brow.

"I'm sorry, cariño," he said. "I have to go home. My father is ill. I have to be there. I have business to attend to."

Her heart dipped. "I'm sorry," she said, her hand flying to her mouth. "I do hope he's all right."

Carlos shrugged. "It's his heart. Too much good living. I'm sorry to leave you though." Warmth returned to his eyes as he gazed at her. "You could come with me. He'd be glad to see you." He glanced around. "You don't have to stay here."

A sudden memory of sunny days filled with laughter came to mind. It would be so easy... Then she remembered Maria and the vision faded. She took a breath. "Please give him my love and hopes for a speedy recovery."

Carlos smiled. "Of course." He sighed. "You know there will always be a place for you here," he took her hand and held it against his heart. "If ever you wish to return."

Again the memory tugged at her heart. She shook her head, but tears welled up in her eyes. How she wished she could turn the clock back, but that was never to be. Maria would always be there, between them. "My place is here," she said.

"Of course. Family I understand." He took her in his arms and she breathed in the smell of him hoping to hold on to it forever as the warmth of his kiss spread through her like melting butter.

"If ever you change your mind…" His eyes twinkled as he got into the taxi, then he was gone and part of Jessie's heart went with him.

Over the next few days Carlos was all she could think about. She emailed Isabella, the Rodriguez's housekeeper, to ask after his father, but really hoping to hear news of him when she replied. She hadn't realised how much she'd come to rely on him around the stables. The extra hand she'd taken on couldn't make up for the loss of his experience and judgement, his light-hearted banter and how problems melted away when he was there. He'd been a huge presence, not easily ignored. The squabbles and arguments they'd had now seemed petty and irrelevant. She'd become so used to his making decisions she felt like a like a feather in the wind, drifting without direction. What had seemed a busy thriving place buzzing with opportunity, felt bereft and empty. She'd let him into her life again and now he was gone, and her heart broke for the second time.

The evenings were the worst. She found herself wandering from room to room, often ending up in what she still thought of as her father's study. She'd sit at his large mahogany desk and miss him all over again. What would he think of her turning the farm into stables? It had been a risk and she couldn't have done it without Carlos's help. That thought brought another ache of sorrow at his leaving. Then she remembered his cavalier attitude when she'd confronted him about his reckless disregard of her plans. Perhaps the memory of the past was cosier than the reality.

Follow your heart, that's what her father would say, but that would only lead to pain. She could never reconcile herself to being Carlos's 'special friend' and sharing his affection. The thought of being a bitter old spinster didn't appeal either.

She caught a glimpse of her grandfather's face in his picture. He seemed to be laughing at her, so she laughed at herself. "You're right as usual, Grandpa," she said aloud. "No point wallowing in maudlin self-pity." With that she got up and went to the kitchen where she made herself a sandwich and a hot chocolate drink to take to bed with a good book, before she sank deeper into the quicksand of memory.

Over the next week Luke and Lucinda planned the grand opening. They met with the caterers she'd booked months in advance. They had no idea where Netherdean might be and were reluctant to travel so far out of town. Lucinda's interior designers, also booked well in advance, were likewise apprehensive. They battled on as the costs rose to compensate for the inconvenience.

"Perhaps we should have used local suppliers," Luke said, "They know the area, the local dishes, what does well and what doesn't."

Lucinda was horrified. "I can't see a bunch of local yokels providing the sort of spread that'll impress the clientele we're hoping to attract," she said. "Really, Luke, you've become a bit of local yokel yourself."

Luke laughed, but he couldn't see anything wrong with blending in with a community he'd come to respect for their hard work and commitment, unlike a lot of city workers he could name. "But if they're coming to experience 'country life' surely a bit of local produce and activities are what they'll expect to see."

"They'll expect to receive the sort of pampering they get at home," Lucinda said. "Only to a much higher standard." She handed him a folder. "These are the people I've invited. I've included a summary of their businesses, bios and likely interests. If you see anything we can build on please let me know."

Luke flicked through the file. Each page had a picture, a brief biography, an outline of the person's business, size, number of employees, etc., together with a note of interests. He nodded his head as he looked at each one, all high-flyers with prospects. She'd obviously done her homework. He found the women the scariest. "I'm sure you know what you're doing," he said. "I'll leave the invites to you."

Lucinda smiled, her eyes shining with approval. "I've invited a couple of journalists too. They write for the up-market business magazines.

We'll need good reviews if we're to make a success of this."

Luke's heart dipped a little. Lucinda was used to playing for high stakes, but Luke couldn't help worrying about the costs.

Going over the menus she'd prepared was another battle. "We don't see many oysters in Netherdean," he said. "More likely to get steak and kidney pie. Something hearty for the harvesters. Fresh air will give the punters an appetite."

"Clients, Luke. Punters are what you get in betting shops." She shook her head. "You've spent too long in the sticks," she said. "You're turning into one of them."

Luke didn't think that too bad a proposition. Having lived there for a while, away from the rat race and constant urge to do better, be richer, make more money than the next guy, he'd found it quite a change, and a good one too.

Lucinda had arranged for a small ensemble with a wide repertoire, ranging from jazz and swing to modern pop, to play dinner music, followed by several speeches from men in the business community. The main speaker was a respected MP and well-known raconteur, again booked at an exorbitant fee. Once that had been agreed they moved on to the other entertainment they could offer. Luke felt more confident about the outdoor activities they'd lined up for the Sunday.

"Of course, it will be November and the weather might be a problem," he said, "so we need indoor alternatives as well."

"That won't be a problem," Lucinda said. "The people I've invited love to talk about themselves and their business. I don't think we'll have any difficulty getting the speakers to give business seminars if need be, for half their usual fee, given they're already there."

"Business seminars? Extra fees? Not a relaxing country weekend then?"

Lucinda laughed. "It's a Business Centre, Luke. Not a chance to vegetate in a haystack and go to seed."

Is that what I've been doing, Luke thought, his brow furrowed. He was getting a little tired of her constant jibes at his appreciation of a different way of life. Or was she right, he was stagnating? And if he was, was that so bad?

"I don't know, Lucinda," he said. "Do we really need an ice sculpture and a champagne fountain? Can't we have one or the other?"

She gave a heavy sigh of exasperation. "We have to give them an experience they'll tell their friends about. Something extra special and out of this world. It's their recommendations that'll keep us in business for the next ten years. Everything has to be perfect. Nothing left to chance. You do understand that, don't you, Luke?"

"Of course," he said, but it didn't stop him worrying about the cost.

Chapter Fourteen

On Market Day, Jessie went into town to put an advert in the local newspaper for her riding lessons, hacks for hire and Pony Trekking Expeditions. Then she went to the bank. Another job Carlos used to do. In the bank she was surprised to see Mr Watkins, the old manager. She'd heard a rumour that he'd been pushed out to make way for Vincent Sowerbridge, but it seemed he was back.

"Good morning, Jessie," he said. "Good to see you. I've been hearing good things about you and your stables."

Jessie remembered her father's old friend. "It's good to see you too," she said. "I thought you'd retired."

He chuckled. "I had, but I'm helping out, temporarily." He lowered his voice to a whisper. "Apparently the new chap didn't work out. Mr Sowerbridge, I think he was called. Lots of complaints. They had to move him on."

Jessie found herself beaming at the thought of the man who'd tried to get her to sell the farm and failed. "I met him," she said. "I'm not surprised they've moved him on. He didn't seem the sort to do well in a small town like ours."

Mr Watkins nodded. "A bit too progressive I believe. Anyway, how is your business now? Is there anything I can do for you?"

Jessie smiled. It really was good to see old Mr Watkins back where he belonged. "I'm fine, thank, you. I just came in to collect the wages."

"A good little business you've built up there, Jessie. My little granddaughter has riding lessons with you. It's the highlight of her week. And I believe the Rotary Club have booked your horses for the annual Hayride. Your dad would be so proud of you."

Jessie blushed at the thought of her father's pride. Damn it, she thought I'm proud of myself, but kind words from an old family friend didn't hurt. "Yes. Are you coming on the ride? They say it will be better than ever this year."

"Wouldn't miss it for the world," Mr Watkins said.

The Hayride was an annual event to celebrate the bringing in of the harvest, and all the local farmers took part. It began with a procession through the town, and ended in a barn with singing, dancing, games, eating, drinking and various high jinks in the surrounding fields. Farmers vied for the privilege of hosting the revellers. This year Jessie's neighbours, Tom and Mary were playing host and Jessie had agreed to help them out.

This year's Hayride promised to be a joyous event. Even Miguel looked forward to taking part.

"Ah," he said. "Festival. Is good."

The event had taken place for as long as Jessie could remember. When she was young her parents always took part and this year she intended it to be something very special. As well as providing horses for the Rotary Club, she decided to put in her own haywain.

All the stable hands were eager to take part and even old Ned had a smile on his face as they got ready. The horses' harnesses were polished until they shone and the old hay cart had a new coat of bright red paint. The wheels were polished too, streamers and ribbons decorated the sides holding great bunches of cress, and hay bales in the back provided adequate seating. A large painted sign on the front declared it to be The Watercress Farm and Stables. Miguel would drive the wagon and Ned and Jessie would be in the back throwing out bunches of new season cress to the crowds lining the route.

On the day the sun shone and Jessie woke to a golden sunrise, the morning air fresh and clean as she let Lady out into the yard. The cress beds and surrounding fields glistened with morning dew. She took a deep breath. This was the first day of the rest of her life, she thought. She needed to move on. Nothing would be allowed to spoil the day, not even the email she received the previous evening from Isabella. She'd been keeping Jessie updated about Senor Rodriguez's health and the last email contained news of Carlos and Maria's wedding. *Such immense good fortune,* she'd written. *Senor Rodriguez is overjoyed at the match which will bring great happiness. Tomorrow will be a wonderful day, full of blessings.*

Jessie's heart crunched. She sent her best wishes by return, but sickness still churned in her stomach. Closing her laptop felt like closing off a part of her life she no longer had access to. She tried her best to think well of them as she went to bed thinking of all she'd left behind in Spain. When one door closes another opens, her dad used to say. Jessie hoped it was true. A vision of Luke Chambers face popped into her mind. She brushed it away. She'd had her heart broken once, she wasn't about to let it happen again, still it didn't stop her recalling his easy smile, his unhurried charm and the way his eyes had lingered on her longer than necessary when they first met.

The morning was spent getting everything ready for the parade in the afternoon. The atmosphere around the stables was one of excited anticipation. Those who weren't riding in the cart would be walking alongside, handing out the leaflets Jessie had had printed about the sessions the stables offered.

Luke arrived back in Netherdean the day of the Hayride. He decided to have lunch in The Feathers, the best place to hear the local gossip. This particular morning he heard that up at Crossbridge, Mrs Riley was still having trouble with her knees and the doctor could do nothing to help, and that old Mr Hoskins had had to have his dog put down. "Riddled with cancer," someone said. They all commiserated. The state of Ted Birley's pigs also brought some concerned comments.

Their muttered conversations served as an ever-present backdrop as Luke enjoyed his lunch. He only took notice when Jessie Tyler's name came up. Jessie was a popular subject of their conversation.

She'd grown up there, they all knew about her father and her job in Spain.

"I see the Spanish bloke's gone then," someone said.

Luke's ears pricked up.

"If you asks me 'e weren't good enough for her."

"I heard 'e had a bob or two."

"I can't see our Jessie bothering about a meal ticket. She's like her dad, independent."

"Aye. She'll not be on her own for long," predicted another man.

"Got 'er wits about 'er our Jessie," another said. "She can take 'er pick."

"I hear Billy Marks is after her."

"Snowball in hell's chance," someone scoffed, and they all chuckled before moving on to the likelihood of a newly widowed woman in the valley being in the market for a lodger.

Luke sat back and thought about Jessie. He recalled how cross she'd been with Carlos Rodriguez about the horse for the ride out and hope blossomed in his heart.

By afternoon Jessie was so busy with her preparations that all thoughts of Carlos and his bride were pushed to the back of her mind. They vanished completely once the haywain, driven by Miguel, was underway. They followed local school children dancing in the sunshine and waving corn dollies and wheat sheaves in the air, a marching band of local scouts and guides ahead of them.

A good crowd had turned out to cheer and clap as they passed. Jessie's heart swelled at the reception. She saw faces in the crowd she recognised and that made it all the more special. Soon she was humming along to the music that filled the air, people threw streamers and waved. She was soon carried away with the bubbling atmosphere and sheer delight on the faces of the crowd. It was only when they passed the church with a bride and groom standing in the doorway waving, that Carlos's face filled her mind and stabbed at her heart.

After lunch Luke watched the Hayride Parade. Nothing like the parades they had in London, he thought, but everyone seemed to join in the fun. The afternoon had an 'end of term' feel about it, the relaxation after a job well done. An onlooker, he felt like an outsider. This was their party, their well-deserved celebration. Perhaps in time he would be part of it too, but for now he was content to watch.

In the evening all the merrymakers flooded into the designated barn and surrounding fields for the dancing, drinking, games and competitions. All in good spirits a cacophony of noise accompanied them. Jessie helped out behind the bar, happy to be kept busy. Seeing her neighbours, the people she'd grown up with, all having a good time brought a swell of nostalgia. She thought of her mum and dad, how they would have loved the camaraderie of the day. People passing congratulated her on what she'd done with the farm and the stables, bringing a flush of pride to her cheeks. Cries of "Well done," "Good on you girl" and "Congratulations, your dad would be proud," echoed in her ears. Musicians started to play, dancers took to the floor, a caller directed the well-known steps, people milled around talking and laughing joining in with the singing of old favourites. The noisy revelry continued well into the night.

Luke joined several of the local businessmen in the evening at the revelries. They'd insisted that he'd 'have a really good time'. He saw Jessie working behind the bar, working while everyone else was enjoying themselves. She looked just the way she had the first time he'd seen her serving in the market, the same as she looked in his dreams. His heart leapt.

He was about to approach her when he was called away by the local builder who'd worked on the Business Centre and wanted to talk about the opening. Most of the local businessmen had been invited. As the evening wore on he noticed that Jessie was often on her own. She didn't join in the dancing, or the games, but kept working behind the bar.

By early dawn the crowd was thinning, the band had finished playing and the dancers drifted of home. Jessie started clearing up, collecting glasses and picking up litter. The warmth of the previous day had lingered and it was pleasant to be out. She'd wandered quite a way from the barn when someone called her name. She turned to see an inebriated Billy Marks, tottering toward her.

"Jessie Tyler," he slurred when he was close enough to put his arm around her. "I've always fancied you."

She felt his weight heavy on her shoulders. She doubted he'd be on his feet much longer. She decided to humour him. "Thanks, Billy, but you're not my type." She tried to shift his arm and ducked, just as he pulled her closer.

"I heard your bloke dumped you." He leered at her. "Mad sod. I'd never do that. How about it Jessie? You and me?" He leaned so close she felt his beery breath on her face.

Rage flew through Jessie. "Is that what you heard? Well, you heard wrong. He never dumped me I dumped him. And as for you and me..." She tried to wriggle free but he clasped her tighter.

"AWWW, Jessie."

She felt his lips, wet and warm on the side of her face. She pushed him away and as she did so he tried to counteract the push, overdid it, lost his footing and tipped towards her, toppling over, taking her down with him. They landed in a haystack, where he rolled on top of her.

She screamed. "Get off me. Get off."

Luke was about to leave to go home when he saw Jessie with Billy Marks, silhouetted against a lightening sky. His heart dropped to his boots, his stomach knotted. They were standing close, he had his arms around her in a passionate embrace, then they were on the ground. He turned to walk away, not wanting to witness the rest, or intrude upon a private moment.

Then he heard her shout, "Get off me." He rushed to help.

She managed to roll Billy over and scramble to her feet. Her clothes were covered in straw. She was picking some out of her hair when a voice behind her said, "Can I be of any assistance."

She spun round and stared into the cornflower blue eyes of Mr Luke Chambers. Her heart faltered. She didn't know what to say. She felt stupid and clumsy. What must he think of her? "No. No. I'm fine, thanks. It's just Billy he's…" She turned to indicate Billy now lying in the straw, oblivious to what was going on around him.

"Oh. I see."

"He's drunk as a skunk," Jessie said. "I think we'd best leave him to sleep it off." She glanced around. "It's clear and dry. He'll be okay."

Luke smiled. "Perhaps I can walk you home then?"

Warmth flooded through her. "Thank you," she said.

He offered his arm, she took it. "I was sorry to hear about your boyfriend's father's illness," he said. "I expect you miss him?"

Bewildered for a moment Jessie said, "My boyfriend? Oh you mean Carlos? He's my business partner, not my boyfriend." She paused as the memory ran through her mind. "In fact today was his wedding day. He married Señorita Maria Fernandez de Santos." Did that sound as bitter as she thought? "An old family friend," she added. She expected the familiar stab of betrayal but instead felt something like a fizz of freedom. It was something of a relief, she realised.

"Oh. I'm sorry, I thought…"

"It's fine," Jessie said. "What about you? Any romantic involvements on the horizon?"

He chuckled. "Just the one, I hope." He glanced at her, his eyes sparkling. "Oh. You mean Lucinda? She's a lovely girl but not exactly the hearth and home type. She's very good at what she does. I couldn't have got the Centre up and running without her."

Surprised, Jessie said, "Hearth and home? Is that what you're looking for?"

"Oh yes, definitely. Hearth, home, cats, dogs," he paused, and looked speculatively at her, "and possibly, horses."

Walking her home under a harvest moon as the morning sun rose, spreading its light over the fields, Luke wanted to grab the memory of the moment to treasure forever. He'd never felt so at ease with anyone. Talking about their different lives, laughing together, it felt perfect, as though he'd known her all his life. As they turned off the road she caught her foot in a pothole and stumbled. He caught her in his arms. Holding tightly on to her, he didn't want to let her go.

"Oops, sorry," she said gently pulling herself from his grasp. He caught the hint of her perfume and breathed in the scent of hope and infinite possibility. His heart beat even faster.

"I'd like to see you again," he said when they arrived at the farmhouse...

She smiled. "I'd like to see you too."

Then he kissed her, and the world stood still. No kiss had ever tasted so sweet. He knew he wanted to spend the rest of his life with this amazing girl. That was when he decided to marry her.

Chapter Fifteen

Over the next weeks Jessie's mood lightened. Even Ned noticed, remarking to Bob Harris how much happier Jessie seemed to be these days.

"Must be in love," the vet, who'd come to check on Lady, said, with a chuckle.

And he was right, Jessie was in love. Luke Chambers had walked her home after the Hayride and asked if he could see her again. When she said yes, he'd kissed her and for a brief moment she'd been in Heaven.

"I'll come again tomorrow, then," he said, then paused, glancing around at the rising sun, "I mean later today."

And he had seen her again, and again. The rides out together became a regular thing and Luke's face was often seen around the stable yard. They'd go into town together for a drink or a meal. The locals soon came to see them as a couple. If he couldn't see her he'd telephone, or text or send her a small gift, or something to make her smile. She thought about him every day. It was as though the sun had suddenly come out and spread its light over her life, smoothing all her worries away.

One afternoon they rode together up to High Point. "It's beautiful here," he said. "So peaceful."

She smiled and kissed him and they lay looking at the sky. But it made her think. Did he mean compared to the clamorous hustle of his hectic life in London? Did he miss it, the excitement, the buzz of a hectic life?

Later that evening she was mucking out the stable, surrounded by hay and the smell of manure that permeated her hair and clothing, the conversation came to mind. Surely Miss Lucinda Grant was more suited to his lifestyle than she would be?

She stopped and thought about it. She felt cared for. But hadn't Carlos cared for her too? He'd said he loved her and then married someone else, someone his family approved of.

Was Luke the same? His family were wealthy. He often spoke of his father with great affection and respect. Would he be happy to see his only son married to a girl who spent her life in wellington boots, up to her knees in horse manure?

Jessie thought about the glossy painted girl Luke had planned to marry. He must have said he loved her too if he asked her to marry him. She didn't know what had happened there. Was he also nursing a broken heart? Where they two wounded soldiers on the battlefield of life, comforting each other until their hearts mended? She shook her head at the thought.

Being with Luke was wonderful, and she loved him, but was it too good to be true?

She sighed and stabbed the bale of hay she was spreading over the stable floor. Don't get ahead of yourself, girl, she thought. Just enjoy the moment but hold on to your heart. She was afraid to think of the future, but it kept niggling at her brain. What would happen when the Centre opened? Was it a flirtation, a dalliance to fill the time before he could pass his responsibilities on to someone else? Then he could go back to his old life in London. Their romance seemed magical, but then magic is illusion, she had to remember that. I'll just make the most of now, she thought, and hold on to my heart.

November brought a change in the weather. The season of mellow fruitfulness turned to wintry frosts and misty drizzle alternating with heavy rain. The night before the grand opening Luke hardly slept. The caterers were due to arrive by six o'clock. He woke at five, after a restless night. He'd dreamt the Centre had been washed away under a deluge of rain and mud. He shivered at the memory, pushing the thought from his mind. It was only a dream, he told himself, not a premonition.

He got up to stare out into the darkness. The sun wouldn't be up for another couple of hours. He turned to switch on the bedside light. Nothing happened. He swore and reached for his phone, turning the flashlight on. Then he tried the light switch for the room, again nothing happened. His heart sank.

He pulled on his jeans and a thick jumper and went down to the kitchen. It's probably a fuse, he thought. The bleary-eyed estate manager greeted him. "There's no power" he said. "Whole village is out."

Luke's heart sank even further. "Great! That's all we need." He shuddered. "What about the generator. How much power will that give us?" When he'd first looked at the farm, he'd noticed the generator. Apparently, all the farms had them due to the unreliability of the power supply. Luckily his architect had seen its potential and insisted it be updated and upgraded.

"Enough for the kitchen and some lights," the manager said.

"Well, that'll have to do for now."

The manager went to rouse Eddie, the resident electrician and engineer. It took a while to get the generator started but Luke sighed with relief as light flooded the kitchen.

He glanced at the clock. Six o'clock. Where were the caterers?

Jessie woke at five-thirty, thanks to a loud commotion going on in the lane that ran alongside her property.

She hadn't slept well. The constant torrential rain that battered the roof and windows had kept her awake until the early hours. She got up and pulled on some warm clothes. She switched on the light and nothing happened. "Damn," she said. Immediately thoughts of Luke and his grand opening ran through her mind. He'd be devastated if anything went wrong. Her heart raced. She went to find a torch. Outside she went to see what all the noise was about.

She gasped when she saw a huge white truck, its wheels spinning in the mud, outside her gate.

"What the devil...?"

The engine stopped revving and two men got out, one of them cursing loudly. He stopped when he saw Jessie.

"Sorry, love," he said. "We're stuck. Don't suppose you've got a tractor or somat to pull us out?"

Jessie shook her head. "No. Is this the catering for the Centre? It's up there." She pointed to the hill that led to the Centre.

"Rollocks to that!" the man said. "Oops. Sorry, love. Begging your pardon. But there's no way we're going to get up there."

"Nor will anyone else."

Jessie turned to see Ned, who'd just arrived, and was staring at the stuck truck. "Impassable after the rain we've had."

"Can you help us out?" the driver asked. "Give us a push or something?"

"I can put some straw down. That might help the wheels grip," Ned said.

He went to get the straw. Several of the stable lads arrived, having also been woken by the commotion. Once the straw was down, they all got behind the truck and pushed, but again the wheels spun and the truck sunk deeper into the mud.

"You'll have to unload it," Miguel, also woken from his slumber, said. "Then perhaps the horses can pull you out."

The driver sighed, but reluctantly agreed to unload the vehicle. Ned put some boards down behind the truck. With everyone pushing and pulling, several heavy metal cabinets, filled with food, were unloaded and wheeled to sit in the road.

Miguel and Jessie fetched the horses and, with the driver's help, harnessed them to the truck.

Inch by inch, with Ned spreading straw beneath the wheels and Miguel and Jessie urging the horses on, the truck was pulled onto the hard standing in Jessie's yard, just as a harassed Luke Chambers arrived.

Luke immediately grasped the situation. The food for a hundred guests was sitting in the road at the bottom of the hill with no way of getting it up to the Centre. Jessie's heart went out to him. "Can we put some boards down," he suggested.

"For this bit yes, but up the hill? No. they'll just slide down."

"Can we drag the cabinets up the hill?" He knew even as he said it, it was a ridiculous idea.

"Even the horses won't make it up there," Miguel said. "Not with that mud underfoot."

Despair filled Luke's face and his heart. He looked as though the end of the world had come. Jessie supposed that, to him, it had.

"There's the bridle path," Miguel said. "It runs behind the farmhouse and takes a loop up through past the Wilking's place. It's longer but a gentler slope. The horses could make it with the cart."

Luke's face brightened. "Do you think they could?" He looked from Miguel to Jessie and back again.

"It's worth a try," Jessie said.

The stable hands pulled out the hay cart and Miguel harnessed the horses between the shafts. The truck driver and his mate managed to wrestle one of the cabinets onto the back of the cart. Then Miguel and Jessie led the horses along the bridle path and up to the Centre, with a worried looking Luke following on behind. Half-way up the rain poured down again, but it didn't daunt their spirits. It took several journeys, but eventually all the cabinets were delivered.

"I can't thank you enough," Luke said. "You've been marvellous. Now all I have to do is find a way to bring the guests up."

Word of the morning's activities soon spread through the village. Once the locals heard of Luke's predicament they all rushed to help. By the time the first guests were due to arrive, the power had been restored, Luke had changed into his best suit, Jessie, Miguel and the stable lads had the horses harnessed and a wagon, a cart and a dray stood ready to go. They each had awnings against the rain and were decorated with fairy lights and bells, ribbons and bows. A variety of colourful quilts and bedspreads covered the hay bales that served as seats. Three men stood at the entrance to the lane with umbrellas, just in case.

Chapter Sixteen

The first car to arrive was the one carrying Luke's father, Mr Henry Chambers, and Lucinda Grant. Luke stood by the roadside ready to greet them as the limousine drew up. He sprang to open the door. "Welcome to The Cedars Conference and Business Centre," he said.

Henry Chambers got out and glanced around. "What on earth? Is this it?" Puzzlement echoed in his voice and creased his face.

"This way." Luke showed them to the first wagon ready to go. "Bad weather," he said. "But a great innovation, don't you think?"

"Well, I must say it's different." Luke's father shrugged his shoulders and climbed onto the wagon. Lucinda wasn't keen. She wrinkled her nose as though she'd encountered a bad smell. "Honestly, Luke?" she asked.

"Road's impassable. Got to take the scenic route." He grinned at her, his heart pumping. If this didn't work out they were sunk.

She demurred, but climbed onto the wagon. Several other cars arrived and, one by one, the visitors were greeted and escorted to the transport.

"Reminds me of a sleigh ride we took in Switzerland," one guest said. "What a novel idea," said another. Someone else thought it 'very jolly'. Luke was just glad they all arrived safely with their luggage.

Jessie heaved a sigh of relief as the last of the visitors were dropped off. It had taken best part of the day, and she was exhausted. She knew the horses were too.

"I can't thank you enough," Luke said. "I don't know how I'd have managed without you. You must come and meet my father. He'll want to thank you too." His eyes shone with appreciation.

Jessie looked down at her mud-spattered clothes and heavily caked boots. The rain had plastered her hair to her head, raindrops still dripped off her coat. She'd been working with the horses all day. She felt sure her clothes were so smelly, even a curious dog wouldn't sniff them. "Glad to be able to help," she said, proud to have done so. "Perhaps I can come back later, when I've had a chance to see to the horses and change." An image of the little black dress she'd bought especially for the occasion ran through her mind. It had cost a fortune, but looked amazing.

"Surely Miguel can see to the horses, and you look amazing just as you are. Come along. I'm dying to show you around."

Before Jessie could refuse, Miguel stepped forward. "I see to horses," he said. "No trouble."

Luke grinned. "Thank you, Miguel. Please come up when you've finished. You too deserve a reward."

Jessie had no option other than to follow him into the impressive building. This is ridiculous, she thought, aware of her filthy work clothes, and the fact that her feet were leaving muddy prints on the polished parquet.

Luke guided her into the lobby where Lucinda was talking to an elderly man. Jessie guessed him to be Mr Chambers, Senior. Seeing them approach, Lucinda stepped away from him. "I'd better go and see to the guests," she said.

Jessie watched as she disappeared into the next room where a crowd had gathered around the bar drinking free champagne and discussing their unusual arrival.

"Papa, I'd like you to meet Jessie Tyler." Luke's voice was marbled with pride "Without her help this event wouldn't be taking place."

The old man turned, warmth in his eyes. His gaze travelled over her, but he didn't seem at all perturbed by her appearance, or the fact that she was dripping rain and mud onto the floor. "Is that a fact? Then we have much to thank you for." He smiled. "I guess you're the Jessie Tyler my son never stops talking about?"

Bemused Jessie stared at Luke. "Really? All good things I hope."

"The best, I assure you," Luke said, putting his arm around her to pull her closer. She caught the satisfied look on his face and the glint of mirth in his eyes.

"In that case, come with me. I want to show you something."

Luke let her go and Henry Chambers put his arm around her shoulders to lead her to the banqueting hall where tables were laid out for dinner that evening. She saw chandeliers and a surfeit of sparkling glass, silverware and crisp white linen all set out – waiting. She imagined the tables filled with evening-suited guests, their faces wreathed in smiles, as champagne glasses clinked and the murmur of conversation filled the room. She gasped. "It's beautiful."

"Hmm. Good. So you approve?"

"Approve? Me?" She glanced at Luke. "I think it's wonderful."

"Good enough as a venue for the wedding reception?"

"The wedding reception?" Shocked Jessie stared at Luke.

"Aw, Pa." Luke shook his head. "I haven't asked her yet."

"Best get on with it then. You don't want a treasure like Jessie getting away."

Luke sighed. "I'm sorry, Jessie. I was going to wait until we were alone, somewhere more romantic, but…"

He dropped down on one knee and took a small box out of his pocket. When he opened it Jessie saw an exquisite diamond ring, the most beautiful thing she'd ever set eyes on. "Jessie Tyler, I've loved you since the first time I saw you in the market. You fill my thoughts and set my heart on fire. I want to spend the rest of my life with you. Please, would you do me the greatest honour and marry me?" Passion burned in his eyes.

Jessie took a breath. She couldn't believe what was happening. It must be a dream. She'd wake up soon and it would fade away. She almost pinched herself before she gasped "Yes. Yes, please I'd like that very much."

Luke sprung up, took her in his arms and, oblivious of the mud and water now staining his best suit, he kissed her.

"Thank God that's settled," Mr Chambers said, as Luke slipped the ring on her finger. "Now perhaps we can get this shindig on the road."

Jessie chuckled as she watched him walk back towards the bar. Her heart swelled with so much love and happiness, she thought it might burst. She took a breath to capture the moment, then Luke kissed her again and all rational thought washed away.

Chapter Seventeen

Jessie loved May. She loved the blossom on the trees, the bluebells in the woods, May Day celebrations and the first crop of the new watercress season. This day in May was extra special. It was her wedding day.

She rose early, enjoying the comparative silence. Birds chirped their dawn chorus and the sound of the stables coming to life drifted over on the light breeze.

She made herself some coffee, staring at the coffee maker – a constant reminder of her time in Spain. She wouldn't be needing it anymore. When Luke moved in they'd have a new one, and a fully fitted, country kitchen.

She took her coffee into her father's study, the room that would soon be Luke's study. She sat at the mahogany desk and gazed at the familiar family photos on the wall. A picture of her mother still stood in its silver frame in front of her. She picked it up. Memories swirled through her brain. She touched her mother's cheek. "It's all right, Ma," she said. "I've got it sorted. I'm keeping the farm and the stables."

She fingered the horseshoe charm on the necklace her father had given her when she went to Spain, *'to remind you where you come from'*. "I'm home to stay, Dad," she said. "The family heritage is safe. We'll be passing it on to our children, your grandchildren, just as it's been passed on for generations." She sighed and put the picture down.

She loved Luke Chambers with all her heart. When she was with him the world seemed a brighter place and she never wanted to be anywhere else.

Luke paced the floor. Today was his wedding day. His father, and his best man, Mark, had arrived the day before.

"Are you sure you want to stay here, forever?" Mark said, incredulity clear in his voice. "It's miles from anywhere. Won't you miss London?"

Luke shrugged. "Miss what? The noise, the dirt, the grime, the pollution? No I won't miss it a bit. Since I met Jessie all I've ever wanted was to be with her, wherever she goes."

"But it's so isolated. I dread to think what it's like in winter."

Luke laughed. "Well, it's a lot better since we improved the road," he said. "I think we'll survive."

His father was more positive. "It's a good lass you've got there," he said. "Not afraid of hard work and getting her hands dirty. She'll do you proud and I'm looking forward to a hearty brood of grandchildren."

Luke gulped. "Jumping the gun again, Pa. At least let us get married first."

"Ah well, got to look forward, son. You never make owt without looking ahead. Fortune favours the early bird."

Luke didn't think that was quite right, but he nodded.

His father glanced around the bar where they were sitting. "Never thought you'd pull it off," he said. "Thought you'd come running home with your tail between your legs. Thought we'd have to cut our losses and run before it was finished, but I have to hand it to you, you've done a good job."

Luke's chest puffed up with pride. His father couldn't have said anything to please him more.

Luke and Jessie were married in the local church. Jessie wore her mother's wedding dress, re-modelled for the occasion. Six bridesmaids from Jessie's riding school wore pink and carried posies of wood anemones, daisies and watercress. Jessie's bouquet was pink and white peonies with honeysuckle, cornflowers and sprigs of cress. She carried a lucky silver horseshoe.

Ned gave her away, and her heart swelled as she walked down the aisle towards her future. The man she loved waited for her. She saw his steadfastness, loyalty, kindness and compassion. He was everything she'd ever wanted.

He turned his head and smiled. Her heart flipped. She was the luckiest girl in the world.

The small church was crowded, all the villagers had turned out to cheer them on. Clouds of confetti filled the air as the church bells rang out.

After the service they rode in a carriage pulled by six of Jessie's horses, up the winding, tree lined road, to the Cedars Conference and Business Centre where the reception for a hundred people was being held. Unsurprisingly, watercress appeared in several dishes on the wedding breakfast menu.

The festivities went on late into the night, but Jessie was unaware of it. All she knew was that the man she loved was beside her, and he'd be by her side forever.

THE END

Author's Note

The inspiration for this story was a visit to a watercress farm in Hertfordshire as research for my novel *The Watercress Girls*. *The Watercress Farm* started life as a short story submitted to *People's Friend Magazine*. The editor thought there was so much happening in the story she asked if I could expand it to a three part serial, which they published in 2019.

The story nagged at me because I didn't feel it was completely finished, so I revisited it and it became the novella you have just read. I hope you enjoyed it.

All author and publisher proceeds from the sale of this book will be donated to the reSEND CIC Pay it Forward Fund to support parents and carers of children with Special Educational Needs.
Your support and contributions will enable the needs of vulnerable families to be met and help provide Justice and Support for All.

If you wish you can donate here:

https://resend.org.uk/paying-it-forward

About the Author

Kay Seeley is a talented storyteller and bestselling author. Her short stories have been published in women's magazines and short-listed in competitions. She lives in London and loves its history. Her stories are well researched, beautifully written with compelling characters where love triumphs over adversity. Kay writes stories that will capture your heart and leave you wanting more. Often heart-wrenching but always satisfyingly uplifting, her books are perfect for fans of Anna Jacobs, Emma Hornby and Josephine Cox.
Kay is a member of The Alliance of Indie Authors and The Society of Women Writers and Journalists.

If you've read and enjoyed this book please leave a review so other readers can enjoy it too.

Sign up to my newsletter for news about my latest books, free short stories and historical trivia. I'd love to hear from you. www.kayseeleyauthor.com

Acknowledgements

I couldn't have written this book without the support and encouragement of my family and writing friends. I particularly want to thank my daughters Lorraine and Liz for reading it and their helpful suggestions. Mostly I'd like to thank my readers for their continued support and encouragement. Hearing from people who've read and enjoyed my books makes it all worthwhile.

Thank you.

If you've enjoyed this you may also enjoy Kay's other books

Novels

The Water Gypsy
The Watercress Girls
The Guardian Angel

The Hope Series
A Girl Called Hope (Book 1)
A Girl Called Violet (Book 2)
A Girl Called Rose (Book 3)

Fitzroy Hotel Series
One Beat of a Heart
A Troubled Heart
All Kay's novels are also available in Large Print

Box Sets (ebook only)
The Victorian Novels Box Set
The Hope Series Box Set

Short Stories
The Cappuccino Collection
The Summer Stories
The Christmas Stories

Printed in Great Britain
by Amazon

27313813R00076